The Mystical Land of Myrrh

Tales from Somalia

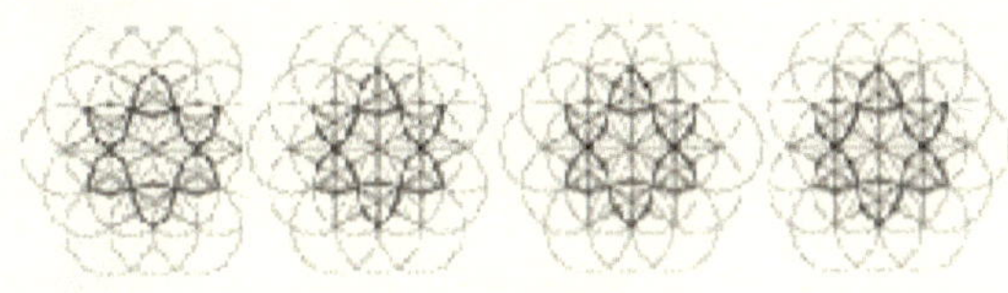

The Mystical Land of Myrrh

Tales from Somalia

by MaryAnn Shank

Dippity Press
Ashland, Oregon

Dippity Press
321 Clay Street, Suite 24
Ashland, Oregon 97520

ISBN 978-1-7335819-0-5

LCCN: 2019900983

The stories in this collection are inspired by my experience, but my memory speaks to me through a fuzzy lens from fifty years ago. Please view all characters in these stories as fiction. Any resemblance to anyone living or dead is purely coincidental. All stories, customs, rituals and ceremonies are ultimately the inventions of the author.

Also note that these stories are not told in a Somali voice. Were a Somali to tell these tales, they would be very different. Even were another Peace Corps Volunteer to tell these stories, even then they would be quite different.

I can only speak from the perspective of a Peace Corps Volunteer like myself, for that is all that I know to be true.

Table of Contents

Map of Somalia

Somalia sits on the horn of Africa, resembling the number "7". It is about the size of California.

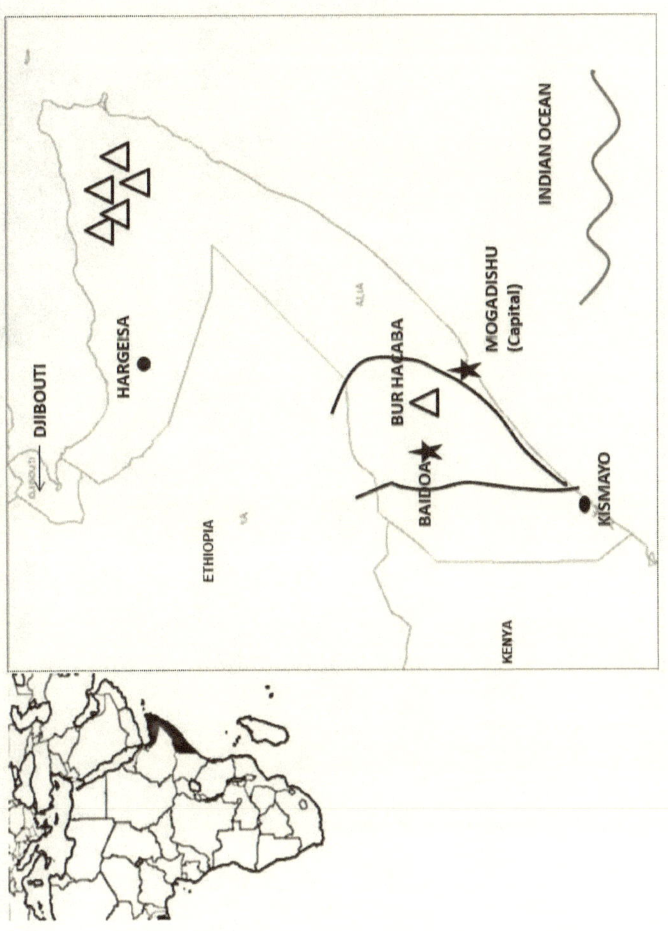

Baidoa, Somalia –
The Last Night

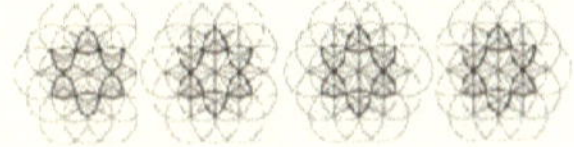

March 22, 1969

THE GRAND GODDESSES played a fiery game of jacks, each tossing an apron full of iridescent jacks, bluewhiteyelloworange jacks, across the pathway of the sky. The Milky Way sometimes glowed so brightly that I could read by its light, mesmerized by the miracle dancing overhead. Tonight the stars skipped between the clouds.

So what was I doing kneeling there in a muddy puddle, the rain obliterating any trace of the tears that tumbled down my face?

"Damn it, stop it!" I shouted to no one. I wanted to taste the salt. I wanted someone to know these tears.

I was so weary of that Howdy Doody smile that all the Peace Corps volunteers wore. I couldn't remember the last time I saw a genuine grin, or heard a giggle. "Did the world still giggle?" I wondered.

So there I was, my last night in Baidoa, my gut twisted in a tourniquet, crying in a mud puddle.

It wasn't supposed to be like this. All the brochures showed angelic young Americans with laughing children at their feet. So many of the Somali children that I knew were too hungry to laugh.

I couldn't laugh either.

They took her away. Shiamsa. Shiamsa, the dedicated, courageous, beautiful young woman who saved my life one starry night. I saw the welts on her shins as they dragged her off. Only her eyes told me good bye.

And Jani is gone too, several months now. She flew out of Djibouti before I could reach her – the interminable rains had washed out the roads, and I couldn't even get out of Baidoa. No roads… No phones… No running water… No electricity… Girls sold for a few stinking camels… Malaria killing over half of all newborns, and most of the rest dying from dysentery… Every single young girl routinely mutilated with a clitorectomy.

"Vile spirits, or whoever you are, what in the name of all the spirits above am I doing here?" My fingernails dug into my palms, crimson spots mingling in the mud.

I rocked back and forth, hoping one of the angels would wrap her arms around me. My fists had been pounding the mud puddle, splashing filth five feet around.

Only a dark silence answered.

The Legend Of Arawello, The Somali Goddess

> *"The women I gravitate to are the ones who defy convention and reinvent themselves - hence, they reinvent the world around them."*
> *Iman, Supermodel, Businesswoman, Good Will Ambassador to the World*

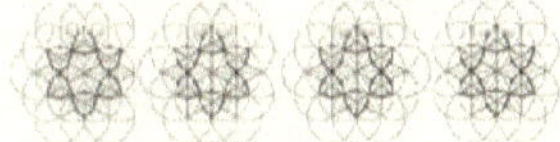

THE RUMORS were true. She did castrate men.

Arawello, the Somali Goddess, was born of Her people. In the first century of the common era Somalia was drowning in a brutal civil war. Bloody decapitations and rotting corpses fed the vermin and the hatred that festered like a vile plague, casting Somalia under a dark death watch. The longer the civil war dragged on, the more pungent the anger and hatred became. Arawello felt the brunt of that anger with fists and whips from the hands of her own father, as had most of the women of the land.

Finally one day Arawello's soul screamed, "ENOUGH! Enough!"

The killing, the butchery, the brutality had to stop. She needed a way to protect her family, protect the women in her village.

First Arawello had to survive.

So in the dark of night Arawello stole away to the mountains of northern Somalia where the aromatic trees grew in what is now the Bari region. The sap of the scraggy *Boswellia sacra* was bled for frankincense, used throughout the Arabic world for medicinal purposes and as a testosterone booster. The thorny *Commiphora myrra* tree was bled for its sap too, a sap called myrrh that was used for healing, for purifying Arab women, and for Egyptian embalming. The sap from both scrub trees was used in sacred ceremonies throughout the Asian region, in all religious sects. These harvested saps brought high prices in the trading ports along the Somali coast, and for those who could tolerate the bitterly cold, dry, windy conditions of the mountains, it provided a rich income.

That is where Arawello went, to the aromatic mountains, where she worked harvesting myrrh from *Commiphora* trees. The thorns of the *Commiphora* pierced her arms by day, but by night she listened to the tales of faraway lands – Sumer, Greece,

Constantinople, China, Egypt, Babylonia and Persia. Traders from around the world brought their stories to Somali shores, and the Somalis who traded directly with the sailor merchants brought these magnificent tales up the mountain, captivating the gatherers on icy cold nights around the fire with hot tea and warm sheep skin blankets.

Arawello met other women, lots of other women, women like herself, women who had escaped the brutality of their villages, and she began forming her plan. Arawello knew that the women who worked the aromatic fields were strong, and determined. She called them together one night and they met by their own fire while Arawello spoke of her plan.

"We will band together. We will train together. We will create an army of women that will bring justice to our villages," Arawello called out to the women.

When the women asked, "How?" Arawello shouted, "We will KILL the men who abuse us!"

A boisterous cheer rose from the circle of women. But one woman stood silent, a bit apart from the others. Arawello saw her.

"My sister," said Arawello, "what troubles you?"

"I watched my daughter being raped by a dozen men. And I could do nothing to stop it," the woman said softly. "My beautiful daughter died. Death is too easy for these men. I want them to suffer as my daughter suffered."

Arawello nodded. She understood.

Arawello thought back to the stories she heard around the fires at night, the stories from China, from Egypt, from Persia and Greece. Some of these stories spoke of eunuchs, of men castrated. The castrated men became obedient servants, for they had nothing left to fight for; their manhood was gone. Arawello could only imagine how intensely they suffered.

Arawello shared her thoughts with the women gathered there that night. "Let us take this night," she said, "and pray. Pray to all the Spirits, to all our grandmothers from generations past. Ask if what we want to do will have their blessing."

So all the women joined hands around the fire and prayed. They shared their sheep skin blankets and passed around cups of boiling hot tea, each taking a turn at refilling all the cups.

In the early grey dawn as the fire began to dim, Arawello asked that every woman who felt in her heart that this was the right path, every such woman should step forward. Every single woman stepped forward without hesitation.

The next few months were rushed with activity. The women pooled their earnings from working the aromatic forests and bought whatever they needed. Arawello hired an Arabic seaman to teach them how to fight, and he purchased precious Arabic swords, enough for each woman to have one. They made their own armor from the hides of the cattle, and carved bows and arrows out of the aromatic tree trunks. They built a fortress for safety and grew their own crops – sorghum, corn, wheat, papaya, mangos.

Queen Arawello stood on a hill one clear morning, overlooking the northern Somali plains, made emerald green from the recent rains. Off to the east were the aromatic forests where the women had first met. All around her was the world that the women had created.

The previous night the women warriors she had trained gathered around a sacred fire, calling upon women from generations past to grant them strength and wisdom. This circle came together every night after each day of training, a day of building new weapons. Rain or sun, they trained with their spears and swords, their knives and bows and arrows, the more advanced warriors training the newer ones. After the sacred circle, the women joined in a communal feast – all taken from their own fields and flocks. Women came and went from Queen Arawello's fortress as they physically and spiritually felt the need. New members typically lived there for several months before going out on a mission, training in military arts, justice and mediation.

On this particular morning Queen Arawello watched as the first groups of women, platoons of three and four warriors, women that she and her lieutenants had trained, fanned out over the entire country.

And, yes, the Queen's warriors did castrate men when they were called upon to do so. The men so emasculated were only those who persisted in lashing out at women and children, a vile habit that had grown out of three generations of brutal civil war in Somalia.

Little by little, village by village, Arawello's army combed the countryside. In the beginning many men were castrated, for they couldn't believe that these simple country women could ever defeat them, and so refused to change their ways. This army of strong women did defeat those arrogant men, handing the reins of power in each village to the women.

The story of Queen Arawello's army spread rapidly, and soon the squadrons of women warriors no longer needed to create peace; they simply needed to maintain the peace with mediation and prayer.

Under Queen Arawello's peace, the whole country flourished. The compassion of the village women became the law of the land, promoting an era of kindness and generosity. Instead of warring, men's energies went into agriculture, husbandry and crafts, leading to a prosperity and abundance that Somalia hadn't seen in many generations. Men and women worked side by side to create a land they had dreamed of for centuries.

Arawello didn't know where the title "Queen" came from. It was just there, and she wore it with dignity. She wore no trappings of royalty, save a golden arm bracelet wrapped around her right arm like a sacred spirit serpent. Her dress, like those of her warriors, was a simple cotton wraparound tied at the left shoulder, with armor made from the hides of their livestock. Some speak of Arawello as the "Queen", and some call her "Goddess". In truth, she may have been both.

SOME TALES say that Queen Arawello was once married and that both her husband and her son were killed in the civil wars. Some tales say she never married. No matter whether she was married or not, no matter whether she was Queen or Goddess, ultimately she was there when Somalia needed her the most.

When Queen Arawello died, a small tomb was built around her grave on the hills of northern Somalia, near where her fortress had been. Only her simple grave remains now. Should you visit it, you may see men angrily throwing rocks at the gravesite, shouting that Queen Arawello never existed. Many men insist on calling Queen Arawello a fantasy. Yet still they throw stones, as if to frighten her away.

Women don't throw stones at the Queen's grave. No, women take small bunches of hand-picked flowers or bits of gay cloth and set them tenderly at the site.

And whenever Somalia is in crisis, Somali women call to the Goddess Arawello, beseeching her to return and restore peace throughout the land.

His Name Was Omar
Chicago

You will be cooled
Walk forward slowly.
Drink it with blessing,
It has no evil.
Your shriveled bones
Are now moist and full again.
("Camel Watering Chant" -- A traditional Somali
song)

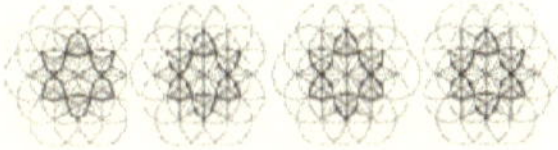

ISCHIA BAIDOA. *The Wells of the People.* Most everyone calls the town Baidoa, but you can still see *Ischia Baidoa* on some old maps.

Baidoa is plunked down in the middle of the southern part of Somalia, in the former Italian territory, midway between the Juba and Shebelle

Rivers. These two rivers flow year-round, pouring across the terrain with a current strong enough to topple a six ton truck, reaching from Ethiopia through southern Somalia. The southern river, the Shebelle, sprints straight to the Indian Ocean. The Juba, the northern river, heads toward Mogadishu, then like a fickle lover it sometimes merges with the Shebelle, and sometimes dissipates into nothingness below Mogadishu, sometimes causing massive flooding. All along their paths both rivers provide water for camels, people and sorghum. They both carry life … and death. The schistosomiasis parasitic worm that flourishes in the Juba and Shebelle rivers destroys kidneys and causes infertility, and sometimes drives unsuspecting animals and people totally insane, even the hippos, crocs and snakes that live there.

At Baidoa the water table bursts through the earth's crust creating natural springs for the year-round population of 5,000 to 10,000, as well as for all the camel trains that can make it there. The camel trains come for water from the springs in the dry seasons, and head off to the bush for lush grazing during the rainy seasons, following the metronome of dry-wet-dry-wet that beats through each year. At the springs, fresh water tumbles over boulders creating spaces for drinking, for camels, for washing laundry, and even a swimming hole for young boys. It is solely because of these springs that the town of Baidoa existed, and even prospered.

WE CAME, four of us, over 120 miles of dirt road, gutted by huge lorries carrying produce and people between Mogadishu and Baidoa. Our five-hour trip in a Land Rover, a comparatively luxurious mode of travel, sprinted and bounced through mile after mile of scraggly thorn bush country, shepherded by our Somali driver. There were no road signs, no directional signs of any kind, but our driver knew the way. Molly and I were the two Peace Corps Volunteers assigned to Baidoa. And there was our driver. The fourth person was Sam, a volunteer stationed in a town closer to the Ethiopian border. We each brought a trunk stuffed with more books than clothes.

Our arrival in Baidoa brought all the bush country surprises I could have hoped for. The thirty or so tiny single-story shops along the main road promised all manner of treasure. They were all square boxes, each under 200 square feet. Back behind the shops on the left I glimpsed the open-air market where individuals put down rugs made of sisal or sorghum stems, setting out hand crafted bowls, wooden spoons, used sandals, fresh papayas, scoops of camel milk, with the meat market of camel and goat meat off to one side. I saw one old woman, her grey dress in shreds, sitting on the ground, no rug of any kind, whose only product was one small can of tomato paste, which she doled out spoon by spoon, earning no more than a few pennies for her day of work.

The village's twenty-foot tall grey obelisk sat at the convergence of three main streets, equally dividing the town into tri-sectors. Our driver knew to take the street to the right, passing the tiny open post office, the one room police station and small government building with bright pink bougainvillea dripping off its sides. Groups of men in long plaid wrap arounds and others in beige slacks parted just enough for our Land Rover to wiggle through, then folded back in behind us, a jagged zipper holding the town together.

Everyone was talking at once, even in groups of four or five men. All were gesticulating wildly, some nearly shouting.

"'Merican!" shouted one man, curling his lip into a sneer and spitting on the ground.

There were shouts about something that I could not even vaguely understand. I had just completed three months of intensive language training in the Somali language, and while I didn't expect to be fluent, I did expect to be able to understand something. I didn't understand a thing, not a silly thing.

"Teacher! Teacher!" A group of five young boys, about twelve years old, ran along beside our Land Rover, waving wildly, smiling broadly. We waved back.

Few women were on the main road that afternoon, and those who were there walked independent of the men, in small groups of two or three women. Their brightly colored wrap around dresses and equally colorful shawls formed a counterpoint against the grey adobe one- and two-story buildings.

Children scampered about too, seemingly unsupervised, but none were doing anything outrageous. Most of the young boys wore beige shorts in various shades of dirty, some with once white cotton shirts. The girls wore miniature versions of their mother's dresses or something akin to a simple American style dress with a high neckline, gathered at the waist.

The whole panorama was a microcosm of what I came to know of Somalia. Much of Somali life was governed by the common phrase *"En sha Allah"* (as Allah wills it), with the acceptance that whatever happens is the will of Allah, and under that was the seething animosity of a country dominated for much too long by foreigners, a people struggling to prove their own worth to the world. This entourage of Somalis captured the feeling of *"En sha Allah"* with an ebb and flow that accommodated everyone, sparked by a vicious desire to make each personal presence known.

I was just settling into this parade of people when our driver turned right again, this time heading in between the tall Catholic church with its ten foot walls on the left, and the Mennonite mission with its grouping of single story buildings including a one-room school and a small clinic on the right. About a mile down this cool tree lined dirt road was Omar Chicago's walkway. Omar Chicago, our landlord and our guardian, stood at the front of a gathering of Somalis.

"Welcome to Baidoa!" Omar Chicago enthusiastically opened his arms wide. The whole entourage – Omar Chicago, his wife, his four sons, his daughter, and about a dozen other relatives – they all engulfed the Land Rover, scurrying to unload our trunks and ensure that we got settled. In the bevy of introductions, I only remembered Yiri's name. She was Omar Chicago's decidedly pregnant wife, and she smiled as broadly as he did.

One man stood a bit apart. "Here," said Omar Chicago. "This is Tifu, your cook!" Tifu became more than our cook. He was the housekeeper, and he did the daily shopping at the morning market, while Molly and I were in school. It seems that Omar Chicago wanted to ensure that a strong man was protecting us, so he brought in Tifu. I was not certain that we needed Tifu's protection, and his cooking left quite a lot to be desired, but Omar Chicago was happy, so we were happy.

For our first meal in Baidoa, Tifu had prepared a big pot of tasteless spaghetti. As we soon discovered, spaghetti was the only thing that Tifu knew how to cook. Omar Chicago, his sons and male relatives joined us for Tifu's spaghetti as Omar Chicago regaled us with tales of life in Baidoa.

We were home; we were in Baidoa, at the Wells of the People.

WHO WERE these people, these people of the wells, the people of Ischia Baidoa? Who were the ones who belonged in Baidoa?

Were the native bushy woolies the People of the Wells? "Bushy wooly" is the inelegant name that westerners gave to brave young warriors from the Rahanweyn tribe who put their eligibility on display with huge Afro style hairdos. These hairdos are so important to the warriors that they don't ever sleep on them. Each Rahanweyn warrior carries a wooden pillow, an intricately carved pedestal with a new moon support where he rests the nape of his neck. These warriors are the only ones in all of Somalia who use these "pillows". These Rahanweyn warriors are typically nomads, the ones the tribe looks to when danger lurks, a responsibility they proudly accept, guarding the several hundred square miles of the Upper Juba region surrounding Baidoa.

How about the women whose kaleidoscope dresses crowd the marketplace every morning? Or the shopkeepers with their white cotton short-sleeved shirts atop beige-khaki pants or redbluegreenorange plaid wraparounds? Or the lorry drivers with their beige and red and plaid turbans, the drivers who are the backbone of all commerce throughout Somalia? Or the beggars in their threadbare garments? Or the naked children who scamper underfoot, belonging to no one and everyone? Most of these people are natives of the region, so surely they are People of the Wells.

What about the old couple who often trudged past our compound, the old man bent over, braced by his walking pole, the old woman following behind, balancing a pile of sticks on her back that was larger than she was, her dress in tatters?

Or the students at the elementary school, or those at Sheik Awes Middle School, or at Padre Vittorio's school? And the teachers? Most of them were from this region, but not all.

Were they all People of the Wells?

Or what about Omar Chicago, our landlord, an anomaly in Somalia, a farmer who had walked the wild sidewalks of Chicago and lived to tell about it? There was no question where Molly and I, the two Peace Corps volunteers in Baidoa, would live; we were to live at Omar Chicago's compound, in the house that Omar built for the Peace Corps volunteers.

Omar's real name was Omar Mohammed Sheik Mohammud, but he wore the name "Omar Chicago" proudly. The term "Sheik" was added to a name when a male Somali completed the Hajj, the ritual trek to Mecca for Moslems. The title is carried for all generations to follow, and it is not unusual to see a name with several "Sheik" titles embedded in it.

"Ten years ago I go to America," Omar Chicago explained. "Twenty Somalis – all farmers. We learn all about American farms."

The Why of this trip escapes me still. Omar, like other successful Somali farmers, farmed with oxen, pulling water by hand out of the Juba and Shebelle rivers, bucketful by bucketful, while U.S. farmers busted their buttons with huge tractors and truckloads full of vile insecticides and chemical fertilizers, and irrigation from abundant water sources.

"First we go to Washington. The big statues! The big parks! The big buildings! Your capital is very big." Omar Chicago smiled slyly as he continued his tale. "Then we go to Chicago. I see movies about gangsters in Chicago, so I go from the hotel to meet them. I see some street signs that say 'Walk,' so I walk. And I see some street signs that say 'Don't walk', so I do not walk – I run. The cars, the horns, everything yells at me. Maybe I come from this way," and he looked to his right, "or from this way," and he looked to his left. He shrugged his shoulders in absolute confusion.

"How did you get back to the hotel?" I asked him.

"A nice lady stop," Omar Chicago said. "She know about the telephone where you put money in. I have a little piece of paper with a phone number. The lady put some money in the phone and call that number. 'Where are you, Omar?' a man's voice ask."

Omar pretended to hold the phone, and looked at it like it was a monster. "'I am in Chicago,' I say. 'Chicago.' That is all I know: I am in Chicago. The man laugh. He laugh and laugh. The lady help, and I go back to the hotel."

"Did you ever see your gangsters?" I had to know.

"No, no gangsters," said Omar Chicago. "Our guide say they gone. But then everyone call me 'Omar Chicago.'" Omar Chicago was grinning ear to ear. He was probably the only Somali to ever go in search of gangsters in Chicago and live to tell about it.

Omar Chicago returned to Baidoa to farm, and, hearing that Peace Corps volunteers would be coming to Baidoa, he built an American style house where Molly and I would live. It was square, about 800 square feet, wooden frame with adobe bricks. Across the back were two plain bedrooms furnished only with two twin beds each, a small bathroom with a long drop toilet and an open shower, and a kitchen with a coal stove. In Somalia there were "short drop" toilets, those with holes in the ground about four to eight feet deep, and "long drop" toilets, those with holes of eight to twelve feet deep. The long drop variety was more luxurious, virtually stench free, and that is the kind that Omar Chicago had dug for us. While most Somalis squatted over a long drop, Omar Chicago mercifully had a western style toilet shipped in for us, as well as a simple ceramic basin for washing our hands. We lived luxuriously!

There was no electricity for a traditional refrigerator, but a modest wood box cooler in the kitchen captured breezes filtered through charcoal.

In the front of the house sat the living room and the dining room. Each room was graced with one window, no glass, but shuttered against the cold rains. There was running water only by virtue of the large barrel Omar Chicago had built onto the roof. That water barrel was re-filled every morning by an old man with a donkey carrying kerosene cans full of water that he had pulled out of the springs a couple of miles away. The old man set up his ladder each morning against the back of the house and carefully carried each can of water up the ladder, dumping it into the barrel. We sometimes got green algae in our shower water, and every drop of water that we drank had to be boiled and filtered, but we had running water, thanks to Omar Chicago's ingenuity.

This modest adobe brick house was in Omar Chicago's compound, just a few feet from his own round hut dwelling that he shared with his wife, Yiri, and their extended family. Omar Chicago's hut was only about one-third the size of our house, but it seemed to expand to include everyone who stopped by, sometimes a dozen or more people. We were on the far outskirts of town with no other houses within a hundred yards. A gentle tree lined dirt lane led past the property, a path I walked hundreds of times over my two year tour, sharing it with camel trains, nomads heading off to the bush and farmers heading to their fields. None of the handy three wheel taxis made it out this far, so we trudged through mud and dust, day after day, along our small path.

WE HAD only been there a few months when Yiri and Omar's newborn daughter met the world. By custom, mother and child were sequestered for forty days after birth. On the forty-first day Omar Chicago knocked gently on our door, and stepping inside, he said most grandly, "My little daughter, Miriam. You show her the world, yes?"

This unique honor could not have evolved from anything either of us had accomplished; it had to have derived from Omar Chicago's immense gratitude to the U.S. for his trip. Whoever was granted the distinction of introducing a child to the world left an indelible impression on the babe – the child's temperament and success derived from the energy of this godmother or godfather style person. While Molly and I stood side by side, introducing tiny Mariam to the wonders of the world around her, I had the good sense to have Molly actually hold her; I didn't want my volatile lesbian energy implanted on this beautiful little girl, for that would have been a curse in the Moslem world.

I held my hands to the sky. I offered a small blessing. "All the Gods and Goddesses and Spirits of all the world, bless this beautiful child. Care for her. Guard her all the days of her life." I held my shawl, softly protecting her from the vibrant sun, as we walked in a circle around all the guests. Then I asked Omar Chicago if he had a blessing too, which he did. Several others stepped forward to offer special blessings as well.

I felt honored, and grateful, and even envious at the ceremony for tiny Mariam. Here was this wonderful family surrounding its newest member, a happy little girl. There must have been thirty or forty extended family members in that circle, all beaming with pride, all eager to help this child grow into the woman she was meant to be. I had no extended family, not like this. My mother knew I was in Somalia, and had even encouraged me to go. I doubted that my father even knew where I was, being far more interested in his next scotch and water than in my whereabouts. I had gone to my father's house to tell him good-by, but he wasn't there. I drove to the local pub and, sure enough, his car was there. I didn't go inside the pub to look for him. My brother was off in Seattle, driving a taxi I think. My brother was incredibly sharp, much sharper than I was, but he couldn't seem to put that intelligence to good use, finding more pleasure in drugs than in food.

But here was this family surrounding us, here in the midst of Somalia. I was blessed to be a part of this family, if only for a few minutes. Songs and dances erupted spontaneously throughout the afternoon.

There was another presence too, a feeling that I couldn't name, a strong protective shield protecting this baby, this family. The feeling was so real that I glanced over my shoulder several times that afternoon, yet never detected any unusual sight. The feeling was neither malevolent nor kind, simply an aura of strength and protection.

Of course there was a feast that day, a young goat slaughtered and roasted over a spit for the occasion, mixed with spices and veggies in a rice dish. It was the most delicious rice meal I had in Somalia my whole two years. We all donned our party clothes, which for me meant wearing a simple pink and lavender dress that a local tailor had made, with an ankle length skirt gathered at the waist. As had become customary, Molly and I were seated with the men on the woven sisal rug on the ground in our front yard, while the women served large bowls of the flavored rice mixed with pieces of the spicy goat, then the women left to eat by themselves.

My long skirt made it easy for me to sit on the rug, while Molly fussed with her short skirt most of the meal, finally giving up entirely and letting her naked thighs show. Baidoa women did not wear a hijab, the long robe that many modern Moslem women wear, covering them from top to bottom. They were dressed in traditional African dresses, long lengths of fabric tied over one shoulder and wrapped around a body three times, with a head scarf and a loose shawl. Being covered as if wearing a hijab was not an issue in Baidoa at that time, but keeping our legs covered to below our knees was a big issue. Peace Corps training taught us that keeping our upper legs covered was a mandatory custom, it was essential. Molly did not observe that custom, as if snubbing her nose at Somali customs entirely. Men and women alike avoided looking at Molly all afternoon, and I felt ashamed to be associated with her. Molly smiled and chattered, oblivious to the insult of her actions.

"Watch me," the Somali man next to me motioned as he scooped up some of the rice and goat dish with two fingers of his right hand. I smiled and did as he instructed, but he needn't have worried, for Molly and I had already mastered the art of eating with just our right hand, rolling the sticky rice into a ball for each bite. It would have been really rude, and shocking, had we used our left hand for eating, for the left hand was used solely for personal hygiene.

OMAR CHICAGO'S SONS took turns guarding our house, all day and night, every day, and that vigilance was justified. Molly and I were curiosities in this patriarchal land, two white women alone in thorn bush country. Some Somalis said that we had come to Somalia because our own families had disowned us, or because we were convicts serving our term. There didn't seem to be any other logical reason why two young women of marriageable age would show up on Baidoa's doorstep. We were indeed curiosities. Some Somalis openly hated Americans, especially American women, those she-devils who led their young girls to corruption. There was some foundation for that hatred of American women. No matter how hard we tried to be modest, everything about us – our clothing, our hair, our voices, our independence – everything – did indeed influence young Somali women and whisper incessantly that they could be more than they ever imagined they could be. In many respects we were indeed the she-devils that many Somalis suspected us to be.

Soon after we arrived, Molly's screams woke me up one night, with bright beams from several flashlights shooting around the bedroom. A group of Somali men had crept up to our window to see what they could see. We had not closed the shutters, for the cooling breeze seemed far more important to us. Omar Chicago came running. He set a second guard at the rear of the house, promising that he would build a fence to protect us. Omar Chicago was good on his word. The next afternoon there was a fence of thorn bushes all around the property. It wasn't the wood fence or chain link fence that I expected, but we never again had trouble with peeping toms.

AND WHAT ABOUT the foreigners? Were we People of the Wells? Did we even belong in Baidoa?

Over twenty foreigners had descended on this village, and another dozen, the agricultural Peace Corps Volunteer contingent, were to come a few months later. Molly and I had a strong mission: to teach English to the governing class so that Somalia could effectively represent itself in the world of politics and economics. A third volunteer, David, had arrived over a year before us, with a goal of building schools in and around Baidoa, building five schools that were truly beautiful, several rungs above traditional Somali construction. There were Mennonite missionaries, a Catholic orphanage and school, Ph.D. level advisors at the agriculture station run by the United States Agency for International Development ("USAID"), Russian advisors for the military base, and even an old Italian ex-pat who kept a cellar full of wines, a treasury that he rarely shared with anyone.

Oddly, the ex pat community in Baidoa never got together, not even once. We rarely talked. Molly and I paid our respects to each of them in turn, some more than others. Padre Vittorio spoke no English, limiting his access to the ex-pats. Luigi, the keeper of the wines, rarely deigned to speak to anyone, and the Russians kept mysteriously to themselves. One of the USAID couples was religiously conservative and socialized with the Mennonite missionaries. But never did we come together to say, "This is my concern. This is what I've learned, and what I'd like to share with you."

The silent arrangement worked fine for me. I served at the pleasure of the country Peace Corps Director who, with but a swipe of his pen, could change my post or ship me home for any reason, or for no reason at all. The Peace Corps, like the U.S. military at the time, was notoriously homophobic, forcing gays and lesbians deeply into dark closets. The extensive FBI investigation that all Peace Corps applicants were subjected to, with FBI agents interviewing our friends, neighbors and professors, was designed to uncloak the "undesirables".

"Oh," my mom told the FBI guy, "I made her the cutest little pink tutus for her ballets. Did you know she was runner up in the Miss Cupertino contest?"

"Oh," my neighbor Cassie told the FBI guy, "she really caught the little boys' eyes."

"Oh," Professor Preston told the FBI guy, "she and that McCullough boy really made a great final project … on the novel 'Tom Jones', as I recall."

So I slipped through the "undesirable" net. Had my family or my professors at college known I was a lesbian, I would have been "de-selected" in a blink.

During Peace Corps training I stayed out of the spotlight, did nothing that focused attention on me, and I made it through. My assignment to Baidoa was the perfect post – it was far enough away from

Mogadishu that the Peace Corps brass pretty much ignored us, and that suited me fine. It was simply too easy for me to slip and say or do something that would throw suspicion on me and get me shipped back to the States, so I did and said as little as possible with the Americans, even Molly. Molly had taught for several years in the States and considered me a dilettante teacher anyway, unworthy of her attention. She taught her students the sanctity of writing in a straight line; frankly I didn't care how they wrote as long as they knew the answer, and goodness knows my blackboard writing was never in a straight line. From my perspective, Molly was just too button up proper to be trustworthy. We mutually kept our distance.

Clinic medics … tavern owners … teachers … military trainers … agriculture experts … orphan care givers … builders of schools … Did any of us belong in Baidoa?

Between everyone else's inclination to build tall fences, and mine, we each cultivated our own private demons and kept them all sequestered, assuming that no one else wanted or needed our help at all. Then, as we each failed, which we all did, we did so privately, with no one there to catch us tumbling down.

I had no idea then how important Somalia would be to my life, how even decades later I would scream at reporters on the telly who ranted about "Somali war lords."

"There are no war lords in Somalia," I screamed back at them. "There are only people protecting their homes. Go home, you damnable invaders! Go home!" The reporters never paused to listen to my woman's voice.

Somalis had settled in my heart. Forever. I readily admit that I still know so little about these wondrous people, but they have captured my imagination and my loyalty like none other.

Stalker in the Sky

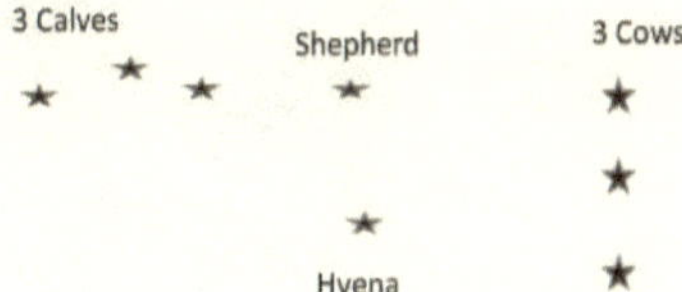

In the northern Somali sky there are three bright stars, a group of cows. Nearby are three smaller stars, calves. In between is the shepherd guarding his herd, and below him is the hyena.

Each night, all over Somalia, young cow herders, shepherds and goat herders scrunch down in their blankets, watching the hyena in the sky creep ever closer to the cows and calves, listening to the sounds of real hyenas and lions nearby.

Maya! Maya!

Auf galad agonta mia?
Maya! Maya!
("Is learning a foreign language enough?
No! No!")
-- Chorus of a popular Somali song in the late
1960s

ABDI, THE HEADMASTER at Sheik Awes Middle School, pointed for me to step outside of the classroom. "Go home," he said sternly, in remarkably good English.

Abdi, like most of the Somali elite – the teachers, the mayor, the police chief – spoke reasonably good English. The Peace Corps had been teaching in Baidoa for five years when I arrived.

Baidoans, like many other Southern Somalis, were fluent at Italian, having been an Italian protectorate for twenty years, but English was still relatively new to them. Somalis in the northern areas were much more comfortable with English, having grown up with the British occupation. Somalis' oral tradition was absolutely unmatched, and a storyteller could recite an epic poem word for word after hearing it only a time or two. With its rich oral tradition, Somalia was known throughout the Middle Eastern world as a nation of poets. They learned some written Arabic, especially when studying the Koran, but the written English word was a whole new challenge for Somali students in the southern regions surrounding Baidoa.

Abdi and I stood in a sun soaked morning, the wispy wind cooling our faces. I wasn't sure what season it was any more. Somalia sits right on the equator, and the alternating dry-wet-dry-wet seasons kept me a bit off kilter. I no sooner got accustomed to eating dust than the afternoon rains bucketed down.

"Go home. Here, sign. Go home." Abdi was flustered, searching for words strong enough. Had he not felt such pressure, his words would have no doubt come much more readily. He held the proctoring sheet out for me to sign.

I was shocked at Abdi's demand that I leave. It had to be a mistake. After all, Abdi was the one who had asked me to proctor the Eighth Forum state exams, and now he was dismissing me like a child being told to stand in the corner for no reason at all. When Molly and I first arrived, Abdi had been there to welcome us. Baidoa had been honored with two American teachers while most communities had none at all, and Abdi was justifiably proud of that.

The first day I stepped into the Eighth Forum classroom, I was surprised by how mature the students were. I was startled when they stood in unison, proudly speaking as one: "Good morning, teacher." This spirited greeting met me every day, in every classroom, and I replied, "Good morning, ladies and gentlemen." We continued that introduction for several weeks until one irritated boy shouted out, "What is this 'ladies and gentlemen'?" So I said it slowly. The word "gentlemen" was already in their vocabulary, and I assured them that "ladies" was the equivalent for girls. They all burst into smiles, boys and girls alike.

"Teacher" (*"ma'alimud"* in Somali) was an honored title throughout Somalia, used by shopkeepers, merchants, and strangers alike when addressing me. All were acknowledging my status as an educated person. *"Nabud mia, ma'alimud?"* ("Is there peace, teacher?"), to which I replied, *"Waa nabud."* ("There is peace.") No matter a person's station or sex, *"Nabud mia?"* was the standard greeting, for peace was the most treasured commodity in a country sometimes overrun with brutality.

It was a full fifty years before I learned how truly kind Bidoans were, for "*Nabud mia?*" was not the proper greeting at all in the Upper Juba Region. It was simply the language that the Peace Corps taught all Somali volunteers, and it did not apply to Baidoa. The language spoken in Baidoa, Af-May May, was as different from Somali as Gaelic is from English. In Baidoa, not only did no one correct me, but they went out of their way to ensure that I understood what they were saying, as though they appreciated whatever feeble attempt at communication I made.

THE FIRST MORNING I stepped into Sheik Awes Middle School, I noticed Musa Barre immediately. He was the kind of student who just stood out. It wasn't just that he proudly wore the uniform of long beige pants and short sleeved white cotton shirt, for all the male students dressed alike. It was a presence he had. Musa Barre took his place in the front row, by the door, as if guarding his charges. At nearly six feet tall, his presence might have given me pause, but his demeanor was calm, sure of himself and his mission. If this school had had a student body president, Musa Barre would have been it. By the end of the first lesson I also got a glimpse of just how really bright this young man was. Musa Barre's brilliant verbal skills matched anything I could throw at him.

"Where is Mogadishu?" I asked Musa Barre.

"In southern Somalia, along the coast on the Indian Ocean," he replied.

"What is the future of Somalia?" I challenged him.

"We will always be a great country," Musa Barre answered, standing tall.

Musa Barre's language structure and vocabulary surpassed anything in my teacher's manual. I was impressed.

Sheik Awes Middle School is the school that the Peace Corps built. David, a tall, muscular blond volunteer, had arrived over a year earlier than Molly and me, and one of his assignments in the construction field was directing the building of this school. The community was rightfully proud of it.

David designed Sheik Awes School with natural stone, molded with cement, four classrooms, all in a neat row, with one door and four windows in each room, absolutely bursting with light, while vents along the roof line allowed for cooling. The vents were truly unique, based on "clerestory windows," open windows with protective eaves from the roof to prevent rain from tumbling into the classrooms. The glassless design allowed for amazing cooling and ventilation, a far cry from the standard classrooms with no windows or ventilation at all. Our teaching jobs were made so much easier by the very clever design that David created.

Each room accommodated fifty to sixty students, and all the classes were jammed full, students shoulder to shoulder, three and four students squeezed onto a bench made for two. The teaching techniques that the Peace Corps taught us in training accommodated the large class sizes and were based on those developed by the Defense Language Institute in Monterey, California. These techniques drew on the natural skills of Somali's oral tradition, with students repeating phrases and sentences after the teacher spoke, then copying those phrases into their notebooks at the end of the class. The verbal approach created exceptional conversational skills. It was so effective that the students in Kismayo, a seaside town just south of Mogadishu, all ended up speaking with lovely southern accents for they had Julia, the Peace Corps teacher from South Carolina.

DURING OUR THREE MONTHS training at Columbia University in New York we had devoted four to six hours a day, six days a week, for three months honing our teaching skills. Everett Iverson, our instructor, was adamant that it didn't matter what else we did in Somalia – if we could teach, we would be respected. In one lesson he even used my teaching style as a "good example," noting that the pace of the lesson was excellent. That bit of recognition probably assured my seat on the Peace Corps Somalia team.

When we weren't learning to teach, we practiced the Somali language. Somali is a diabolical language to western ears, with grammatical constructions and sounds that we had never heard before. English is reputedly a tough language to learn, but at least English sits somewhere on the language tree. Not so Somali. Somali was part of no known language tree, sitting alone on a thorn bush in a forgotten land. On top of that, there was no attempt at all to introduce the five very distinct languages of Somali. We all learned just one of the Somali languages, the one spoken in Hargeisa, the largest city in north Somalia. Our final language exam demanded only that we carry on a two-minute introductory conversation with our name, profession, where from, and common niceties … in a language we would never use.

At the end of our three months of training at Columbia University we were told to evaluate each other, each of us listing the five top candidates in our group, and each of us listing the five worst. We bristled. Good grief, we were a team. All thirty-five of us stood and roared our dissent in unison. We weren't going to evaluate each other like a bunch of livestock on display. The Peace Corps assured us that this evaluation was the best indicator of success that they had, far better than any instructor's appraisal, so in the end we capitulated and we judged each other. With male volunteers out numbering women four to one, and an all-male staff, I didn't know what chance I stood of getting a good ranking.

Then came the dreaded appointment with the psychologist. This was The One who had full authority to kick us off the team, for any reason at all – he didn't even have to justify his actions. I showed up for my appointment with considerable trepidation. Clearly, he was the chief head lopper. His generous form spilled over his leather chair, and his pea shooter eyes peered over horn-rimmed spectacles. His arms weren't long enough to rest on the table, so he draped his arms over the arm rests, his left hand holding a Cross pen poised to draw a line through my name at any moment. The psych's practiced stare bored into my innards. Thankfully, I was adept at diverting arrows aimed at my most private thoughts. Something very deep inside me screamed that I wanted this Peace Corps assignment very badly – I had to go, and no fancy psych was going to break me. I sat tall, ready for the onslaught.

He spoke sweetly authoritarian, befitting one who wants your innermost secrets. "Well," he said. "I see that five people have designated you as one of the best volunteers. That's impressive." I silently thanked Everett Iverson for his endorsement, for that is the only thing that might have prompted such an evaluation.

"I see too that five people have listed you as one of the worst volunteers," noted the psych.

He expected me to respond, but I had no response. I silently stuck pins in the voodoo dolls of the foolish boys who couldn't seem to keep their grubby paws off my boobs and butt. With only six single female volunteers in this group, several male volunteers seemed to think that the female volunteers owed them something, at least a good feel up. I had kneed more than one of them, and here was my pay back. I couldn't complain, though, for I had listed them on my "Worst Volunteer" list too.

"You do seem to make an impression," the psych said.

"Yes, sir." I couldn't even begin to explain anything else to him, let alone why those blasted boys just weren't my type. Any hint of my lesbian background would have sent his pen to flight, obliterating my name from the list forever. So I simply shrugged a bit.

"Why do you think that happened?" he insisted.

I mentioned Everett's comment, and noted too that perfection just wasn't my strong suit. He wrote something in his notebook, paused, then asked, "What do you think of Jerry Hammerling? You mentioned him as a Bad Volunteer."

Indeed I had. Jerry was one of the ass grabbers. "Well," I said carefully, "Jerry seemed to have trouble learning Somali, and I thought he might have difficulty communicating." I shook my head sadly. The psych wrote something else in his book.

"And Gettner … Louis Gettner? What do you think of him?"

Everyone thought Lou was gay. Did the psych already have my number, or was he just taunting me? I straightened my back like it was just the question I wanted. "I like his teaching style," I said. "He's got a great pace in his lessons."

When the assignment list came out a few days later, Lou Gettner was not on it. I hadn't seen Lou for a couple of days, rumors being that he had been "de-selected". I made it, and so did all of the ass grabbers. It was a lily-white group chosen by men: no blacks, no Jews, no Asians, no homos, no one religious enough to want to attend church on Sunday. There was no one too fat, or too skinny, or too hairy. The women were all pretty, and bright shiny scrubbed faces glistened in our group photo. We were the perfect sliver of white middle class America. We were so perfect as a group that none of us even mentioned how ultra-homogenized we were – no one, not even me. The FBI investigations and whole selection process had been programmed to identify this perfect little group.

I was assigned to Baidoa.

THE ROOMS AT Sheik Awes Middle School were barren except for the desks and benches, and one large plywood display board on the back wall. I tacked up a large map of Africa in one of the rooms, with zebras and hippos and monkeys and lions all along the sides. The kids loved it.

There were only eight to ten girls in each class of sixty students. The girls spoke softly when I called upon them, and they never volunteered to speak. Girls were not accustomed to speaking up in a mixed group of boys and girls, so it was tough getting them to participate in class. It wasn't that the girls were shy, it was just part of their culture. On top of that, I wanted to respect their customs, so I didn't want to force them to participate. Yet when I did call upon them, they nearly always knew the answer. They were exceptionally bright young women. I felt proud that I was helping to prepare them as teachers, as leaders in the community.

Each morning I saw the young women gathered, similar billowing white cotton dresses standing apart from the boys. The simple white European style dresses with high round necklines, cap sleeves and gathered skirts that came almost to their ankles spoke to their modesty. The sky blue stripe near the hem and demure blue or white head scarf knotted at the nape of the neck reflected the blue and white colors in the Somali flag that flew in the courtyard. Fatuma, one of the brightest young women, always stood outside the circle of friends, composed, waiting for school to start.

Sometimes I wandered over for a brief conversation with my girls before school started.

"Where do you live?" I asked Aisha, one of the older students. The names were summer breeze lyrical: Aisha, Miriam, Fatuma. Very few names were used, even with the boys, so everyone used their father's name and their grandfather's name too. Aisha Abdi Omar and Aisha Abdi Mohammud were both my students. When a young woman married, one of her first tasks was to learn the whole genealogy of her husband, all the way back to Mohammed, so she could teach it to their children. It was the bride's mother-in-law who typically taught this genealogy to her.

"There," said Aisha, pointing to the village.

"Do you have brothers and sisters?"

"Yes."

Yet when I asked the girls if they wanted to be teachers, their eyes lit up. "Yes! a teacher!" A chorus of pure enthusiasm rang out from all the girls at once.

Being an elementary teacher was the highest goal permitted for women in Somali culture. A few poor women sold modest goods in the outdoor marketplace, and a few were waitresses in the tea cafes, but the status of teacher was one to be envied. Teachers might only teach a few years, until they got married and began having children, but the girls worked hard to make that dream come true. Simply by being in school they were building new ladders for

Somali women, and I wanted so badly to help them succeed.

Students ranged in age from about twelve to about eighteen, sometimes all in the same classroom. Students began school when their family decided to send them, when their families could afford the tuition, not at any particular age. Most were selected by their families to be the leaders of their generation. These were good kids, hard-working students who appreciated their privileged status. I was pleased that whenever I went into the village a few of my students appeared from nowhere and escorted me, showing me their favorite shops and translating for me.

THERE WAS ONE DAY when Abdullahi Sheik Mohammud called out to me as I left the tea cafe in the village. "Teacher! Teacher!" he called out, "Come. Here is my uncle!"

I liked Abdullahi immensely; even when he didn't know the answer in school he wore a huge smile. I followed Abdullahi to his uncle's shop, a tiny room stuffed with bolts of exotic fabric from Egypt and India. I picked out a vibrant green and yellow geometric design with triangles and bold lines intersecting, and I drew a quick sketch of the muumuu style dress I wanted. For about two dollars the dress was ready for me the following day.

THOSE FIRST FEW MONTHS I enjoyed teaching at Sheik Awes Middle School. The only real glitch was the cheating issue. When I gave the very first written quiz, the students brazenly cheated. Nearly all of them cheated. They passed their papers around and spoke with each other in loud whispers. I tried quieting them, to absolutely no avail. I let that quiz go, and relied instead on oral quizzes, which I could better control.

Then came the state exam.

The state exam was important. It would determine who would, and who would not, be invited to attend the high school in Mogadishu, the only secondary school in the entire country. Only the country's finest young people, those with exceptional intelligence and remarkable family heritage, were invited to attend, and those selected were destined to be the future leaders of Somalia. A very honored few of the secondary school students would continue their higher education in England, Egypt, Turkey or the U.S., perhaps becoming engineers, doctors or business leaders. Those with sufficient popular backing became legislators and headed the Somali cabinet, the democratic system that the Allies had foisted upon Somalia after World War II. Prior to World War II, Somali society was built around communal tribes with no borders, a society of both cooperation and competition. The tribal society had served them well for centuries.

But the Allies had decided that Somalia should be a centralized democracy with well-defined borders, and now graduation from the secondary school was a prerequisite to leadership of the country. Sadly, there was no test for integrity, and that was the keystone to leadership in the old Somalia. The new-fangled tests measured only school learning, leaving behind many who were natural leaders, promoting others whose knowledge came only from books.

I tackled my proctoring assignment with all the fervor of proctoring college entrance exams, for that is truly what it was and I knew exactly what to do; I had learned a lot during those first few months.

The girls always sat in the back of the classroom by themselves, squeezing four or five onto each bench. I knew that the boys wouldn't be so tempted to cheat if a girl were next to them, for physical contact between boys and girls was strictly forbidden. So before I handed out the tests, I rearranged the seating and put a girl in between two boys on nearly every bench. The girls had their eyes to their laps, their arms scrunched against their bodies as tight as they could. The boys openly glared at me – Ali Mohamoud, Yossi Sheik Hassan, good boys -- openly sneered at me, their lips curling into nasty threats, as they balanced precariously on the edge of the benches.

"No, teacher," Musa Barre protested. I simply ignored him.

No sooner had I handed out the exams than Musa Barre bolted out the door, returning moments later with Abdi. Abdi motioned for me to follow him outside. Clearly, Abdi was not kidding.

"I won't go home," I said quietly. "I have a job to do." I straightened my back and took a defiant step back toward the classroom. Abdi's arms shot out, blocking my way. "Oh no!" I thought. "He will even risk full body contact before he will let me back in that classroom."

"Go home." His voice was slow and deliberate as he held the proctoring sheet out to me. He risked no misinterpretation. I took the proctor sheet, signed it, turned around and, standing as tall as I could, I walked deliberately in the direction of the road home. My brain swirled. What went wrong? What had I done? How can a day that was so fresh and sunny turn so miserable? What had Musa Barre told Abdi? Was I to leave Baidoa completely? Why was I summarily dismissed?

Ironically, as I reached the edge of the school yard, the cool breeze that had softened the sun abruptly stopped. I walked the rest of the way home sweaty, in silence. A door had slammed shut behind me.

I wasn't sure if Abdi's admonition to "go home" meant I should go back to Omar Chicago's compound, or if I should go back to the United States. I chose to stay in Baidoa. I went back to school the next day and taught just as I had before. No one said anything. That was the trouble: no one said anything. The warm, professional demeanor that had defined my relationship with the Somali teachers and students became an icy wall that I couldn't break through.

As I entered the Eighth Forum the next morning, all eyes turned to Musa Barre. He stood. They all stood. As he began, "Good morning, teacher," they all joined in. But this wasn't the enthusiastic greeting of the first day. It was a flat statement that haunted me the rest of my tour in Baidoa. The tempo of the class, once a lively trot, fell to a muddy slog.

When I took a walk into the village that afternoon, I saw a number of my students, as usual. But now they disappeared behind buildings or merged into a larger group. None of them came to escort me. All but Musa Barre. He did not disappear. Nor did he greet me. He simply stood outside one of the shops and watched a group of men about twenty yards away. When I moved a few shops further down, Musa Barre moved too, silently, still not acknowledging me. I felt a chilly sweat dripping down my face. At first I thought this was part of the growing discontent in Somalia, especially with the anti-American contingent, but when my students disappeared I knew it was something else entirely, perhaps something in addition to the anti-American sentiment. I motioned to one of the three wheeled taxis nearby, telling the driver I wanted to go to Omar

Chicago's house. The taxi driver glanced at Musa Barre, and Musa Barre nodded ever so slightly. As the taxi sped away, Musa Barre was still looking off in the distance at the group behind me. The next day Musa Barre told me to not go into the village alone. He didn't have to tell me why.

LIFE CONTINUED in Baidoa, pretty much like that. I was blocked out, shut off, transformed into a *persona non grata*. I was allowed to remain only by the grace of Allah. The Peace Corps in Mogadishu never learned of this incident, or if they did learn of it, they didn't care.

My only true refuge was when I entered the Catholic orphanage each afternoon. This is the orphanage that the Italians had built to accommodate some of the Italian-Somali half-breed children that the Italian soldiers had left behind, the total outcasts of Somali society. The two Italian orphanages in Somalia -- one for boys here in Baidoa, and one for girls in Kismayo on the coast -- could accommodate but a few of the outcast children; the rest were left to fend for themselves in a hostile society. Most of these mixed breed children died a sad lonely death, alone in alleyways or wandering in the bush – no food, no water, and barely a rag for their backs. Those boys who were rescued by Padre Vittorio were blessed indeed. He had taken it upon himself to scour the gutters and back alleys for these forsaken boys, and took them to Baidoa where he housed them and fed them, and gave them an education.

We hadn't been in Baidoa a week when Padre Vittorio knocked on our door one afternoon. The good Padre couldn't speak English, so he had recruited a policeman to come along and interpret. While the policeman's English wasn't great, the gist of the message was that the Padre desperately wanted someone to come and teach his boys English. Every afternoon, please. Except Fridays and Sundays. On Fridays the boys went to the mosque, and on Sundays they went to mass. I had hoped to get involved in a project with local girls in the afternoons, but the Padre's eyes spoke with such immense compassion that I said Yes.

So every afternoon, except Fridays and Sundays, I knocked at the thick ten foot high wood gate of the Catholic mission, and it was always promptly opened by a smiling nun or youngster. I think they had someone stationed by that gate so I wouldn't be kept waiting. Stepping inside I was transported to a little paradise all its own. Red roses and white lilies bloomed all over, with all manner of exotic flowers and even ferns and a glorious grape arbor. The grapes, succulent morsels that popped sweet nectar to your tongue, were relished by the students as coveted rewards for outstanding work. This was a home that Padre Vittorio and the five nuns tended with immense love. With drops of water so precious, I could only imagine how they cherished each plant. Padre Vittorio joked that Somalis thought he was very wealthy because he had five wives.

And there was a seventh Italian, Mario, a slender, handsome young man in his mid-twenties who was volunteering to help at the orphanage, much like a Peace Corps volunteer. Mario didn't speak English either. But Mario spoke some French, and I spoke some French. So that is how we conversed. When Padre Vittorio or the nuns wished to say something, Mario translated it into French for me, and we went the other way around when I wished to speak. Accuracy in communication was not our strong suit, but sincerity certainly was.

Teaching these boys was such a joy. All of the sixty or so boys, all elementary grades, crowded into one room so they could all learn. Padre Vittorio and Mario were there too, and sometimes I saw a nun's black habit sneak behind the bushes by the windows. This was the Peace Corps that I had been looking for, happy smiles and laughter, and students so eager to learn that I had a hard time keeping up with them.

The Padre knew that his boys were outcasts in Somali society, half breeds scorned by everyone, and that their only hope for ever earning a living was to learn English. With English skills they could become translators and interpreters, or perhaps even teachers. No matter what they did, this one skill would be in demand, and they would have it. English was to be their passport to a secure future, and I felt so proud to be able to help. Padre Vittorio also ensured that all the boys kept their Moslem traditions, arranging for an *iman*, a religious man, to teach them every morning, just like other young Somali boys. The *iman* arrived each morning with a chalk board taller than he was. He wrote an Arabic phrase on the board, something from the Koran, and the boys memorized it, just as boys did all over Somalia.

Had it not been for these orphans, I would have left Baidoa after the state exam incident, but I just couldn't leave my boys. They truly needed what I could teach them. I did note that after that incident I no longer walked the half mile to the orphanage alone. Every single day two or three of the older boys from the orphanage met me at my doorstep, waiting to escort me to their school. And I was glad for their company. I had not spoken to Padre Vittorio about the incident, but he had been in Baidoa over two decades and had developed good sources of information.

The state exam incident haunted me, way out of proportion to its importance, I thought. A couple of weeks later my friend Alan, the Peace Corps teacher assigned to Beledweyne, a town about fifty miles away, came down for a visit. I asked Alan if he had proctored the state exams.

"Sure," Alan grinned. "All the teachers proctored the exams."

"All?"

"Yep. We all sat outside in the courtyard, drinking tea. Then one of the teachers brought out a copy of the exam, and we all tried to figure out what the best answer might be. Some of them came up with hilarious stuff. It was a fun morning."

Had Alan facilitated cheating at his school? Probably. But I said nothing to him about it.

MY BAIDOA DAYS passed slowly. Some evenings I sat on our little patio, watching the camel trains head off into the bush country, outlined by the bursting setting sun. Camels were made for thorn bush country, with four stomachs that devoured tons of thorns and turned those thorns into milk. I was awed that camel herders could go off into the bush country, never knowing if the next water hole would even be there. *"En sha Allah"*, they always said. "As Allah wills it." In a few days they would meet another camel train of their own tribe and together they would trade information about the status of water holes and any lurking dangers. With all of their combined knowledge, they made it through many very tough droughts and horrendous rainy seasons. They made it through together.

They made it through together.

Gradually the severity of my stupidity sank in. How could I have been so dense? The students weren't cheating at all. They were making it through together.

Most of the students at Sheik Awes Middle School were from the Upper Juba region, and were of the same tribe. This was their middle school, their only middle school. If the communal tribe wanted to be represented in higher government and have opportunities for lucrative positions and national power, then these students had to succeed. There was immense pressure on them to do well in the state exams. The more students who went to Mogadishu to high school, the stronger the tribe would be in the country's future. Education was not free in Somalia. Families paid dearly to have their most gifted children educated, boys and girls. The payoff to the families, and the tribes, was stronger influence in governing the country.

So here was this smart ass young American woman who was making all that investment wash away like water off a donkey's back.

There was a greater impact from these exams too. While someone like Musa Barre would likely pass the exam on his own, if he intended to be a strong leader in Somalia, he needed as many others from his tribe as possible to rise with him. He needed his wing men, and lots of them.

Truly, it really didn't matter a whole lot what they learned in school. It did matter – a lot – that they passed the state exam, no matter how; hence the communal effort at passing the exams with exceptionally high marks. The state test was in

English, and they were depending on me to help them. They were competing with every Eighth Forum student throughout the country, even hundreds of students in northern Somalia, students who had been raised under British rule and had spoken English since birth. Most of my students had learned Italian as young children, not English. They had turned to me for help. Everyone knew they had an exceptionally strong group of candidates. All they needed was some help over the hump. Not only did I turn away, but I tried to tie their hands behind their backs.

I felt sick, miserably sick at heart. I seriously wondered why we were trying to foist western ways on these people. Individual accomplishment may have worked in the western world, but communal success was so much more critical in this world.

I tried apologizing to Headmaster Abdi and to Musa Barre. "It is over," is all Abdi said. He didn't speak in anger or in acceptance; he just spoke, then walked away.

"*En shah Allah*" (as Allah wills it) was all that Musa Barre would say. Then he too turned and walked away.

A few weeks later I learned that no one from Baidoa had been selected to attend high school in Mogadishu. No one. Not Musa Barre, none of my girls. It felt like a bowling ball had pummeled into my gut. That did it. I made Molly promise that she would teach at the orphanage at least three days a week, I packed my trunk, and I caught the next lorry into Mogadishu. I don't think shock absorbers had reached Somalia yet, so even though I was given the seat of honor up front with the driver, it was a horrendously bumpy six hour ride. The road between Baidoa and Mogadishu was nothing more than a one lane dirt road, gutted with pot holes whenever it rained, pot holes that were never completely filled in. The ruts in the road looked like a turbulent eddy, with no sense of direction at all.

When I arrived in Mogadishu I marched immediately up to Jack Connor's office. As the country Peace Corps Director, Jack would understand my situation and be able to help. He looked tired, weary of balancing demands from Washington, the Somali Department of Education and USAID people who didn't much like these Peace Corps do-gooders. I made my story short. I begged for another post, a place where I could forget the blunders I had made and start over.

"Fat chance," said Jack in his none too mild voice. "There are no other posts available. Get back to Baidoa and do your job." Jack let loose a slew of vindictives, an easy task on his tongue. "Can't you just get along?"

"Just get along." So that was the deal. Here I had imagined I was in Baidoa to help the next generation of Somalis step up to world leadership, giving them a command of English, math and science that they would never have had otherwise. No, all that Washington wanted was for us to "just get along."

"Just get along." No, that had never been my strong suit. My stubborn streak had disrupted more than one relationship. Even Willow, my girl friend back home, refused to wait for me while I went to the Peace Corps, saying I was much too intent on saving the world. I was.

I got soused that night on cheap red wine at the Italian bar at the Shebelle Hotel, served by the Somali bar tender. Although Somalis were strictly Moslem and would not touch liquor, they knew that foreigners were different and allowed us the luxury of beer and wine at the only large hotel in Mogadishu. No Somali would have been served at the hotel bar, but I was. Alone at the six seater bar, I weighed my options. I could be sent home in disgrace, forfeiting even the seventy-five dollar per month stipend that the Peace Corps gave us, or I could go back to Baidoa.

The next morning I had a gut wrenching hangover worthy of the red rot gut, and that afternoon, my stomach still lunging from the cheap wine, I lugged my trunk back to the market area where lorries, vans and buses converged, gathering passengers. When enough passengers wanted to go somewhere, the driver loaded up and headed off. The produce lorries attracted swarms of flies and mosquitoes. Somalis seemed immune to these vermin, but I wasn't; they irritated the dickens out of me.

I got the last available seat in a ten seater van heading back to Baidoa. The driver was half mad, likely the result of his having spent the morning at a q'at club where men chewed on the disgusting weed, something akin to an opium den. The driver's zig zagging was seemingly intent on hitting every pot hole possible, each jolt dragging me deeper into my own private undertow. Drat it! my period started about an hour into the trip. The vicious jolting of the bus shook all five days of menstrual flow out of me during that six hour ride. The few Kleenexes that I had on hand were woefully inadequate, and there were no stops for women along the way. The only stop was to allow men to head off to the bushes to piss. With sweat pouring off my face, I tore a strip of fabric from my head scarf and wound it into a pitiful tampon. There was one other woman on the bus, a young Somali woman, who mercifully held her shawl so I had a bit of privacy to push my meager wad in place. With the bus jolting profusely, I stuck my filthy finger with the wad up my vagina.

It was a hot gooey afternoon and everyone opened wide all the windows in the van. We had hoped for a breeze, but pools of sweat only glued the red dust clouds to our skins making us hotter by the hour. Salty muddy sweat stung my eyes and jolted me out of a jagged reverie, the one where I had caught an exotic disease and had to spend the rest of my tour in Paris, with very accommodating nurses tending to my every wish. Startled awake, I felt that stiff wad sawing my clit. The first few layers of blood had dried so hard in the heat that the blasted wad became a vicious serrated edge, cutting into me.

BY THE TIME I got back to Baidoa I stunk from blood and sweat and filth. I didn't have the heart to put my pile of stench in one of the three wheel taxis still roaming around, so I put the trunk in one, paid the driver to take it to Omar Chicago's house, then trudged the two miles alone, as if doing penance. It was dark, and no one saw me.

The next day I went back to work. No one said a word.

The chill, however, persisted. It is hard to define a shunning until you see backs turning toward you wherever you go. A couple of weeks later I went to talk with David, the Peace Corps Volunteer constructing schools, about the whole mess. He had been in Somalia the longest and seemed sensitive to Somali ways.

"Don't worry about it," David assured me. "All the locals have to do is pay extra *bakshish* to have their students admitted in Mogadishu."

David was right, of course. *Bakshish* – the bribe for every occasion – *bakshish* was the great leveler. *Bakshish* was ingrained in Somali life, in the construction area where David worked, and all throughout government. Westerners held their noses when they spoke of *bakshish*, as if it were a dirty word.

I saw it only as a way of doing business. In the West, politicians were bribed with all manner of currency, with special favors and discounts, and we all accepted it as a way of doing business. In Somalia the *bakshish* was something of a leveler, a way of spreading the wealth from the very wealthy to the middle classes. Enough *bakshish* could buy anything in Somalia, and it could certainly buy entry to secondary school in Mogadishu.

Ultimately my blundering only accomplished two things: it cost the local tribe extra *bakshish* to get their students admitted to the secondary school, and it kept my girls from proceeding with their education – no one was going to pay *bakshish* for a girl's education. Sadly, the fate of my girls was sealed.

My fate was sealed too. I had lost the honor and respect of being a teacher, and I would never again be called upon to help them make it through together. That door had slammed shut behind me. I had become a financial liability. Ironically, it was probably *bakshish* that earned Baidoa two American teachers in the first place. Now, cloaked in cold anonymity, I went through the motions of teaching, day after day. The following year when it was time for the state exams, Abdi told me it was a special holiday at school and he sent over a government official to take Molly and me for a picnic in the bush… as far away from Sheik Awes Middle School as possible.

Auf galad agonta mia? Was teaching a foreign language enough? Was book learning enough?

Maya! Maya! No. By all the spirits above, No! not by a long shot.

The Never Ending Tale

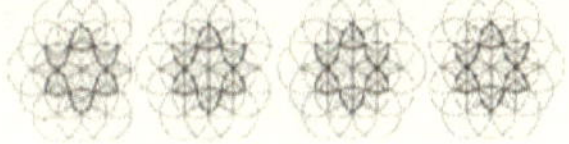

"OH, MORIAH, I am so glad you are okay." The gaunt wife of the senior USAID person in Baidoa caught me as I stopped by the Mennonite mission to thank them for helping Molly when I was out of town. I came close to hating this woman. I certainly detested her. She wallowed in shallow gossip and had turned a personal put down into an art form. Her scrunched up nose made her look like a hog, and to me she was always Hog Face.

"Yes, ma'am, I'm fine, thank you," and I turned to leave, hoping to escape her next sentence, but I wasn't fast enough.

"There are reports that a Peace Corps Volunteer, a red head, was raped in Mogadishu, and I thought of you," said Hog Face. "You have to be very careful around Somalis, but you know that. And you never go out alone at night, do you, dear?" [Translation: "I just want to scare the shit out of you, sweetie."]

This stupid rumor had a life of its own, popping up several times over my two-year tour, and it was always a red head in Mogadishu. There was only one other red head in the Peace Corps and we were both fine, thank you very much. It was invariably Hog Face who kept me informed of these rumors.

Shiamsa in Shadows

Until I die I shall not give up my song of love,
Oh, God, forgive me my weakness.
(Traditional Somali folk song)

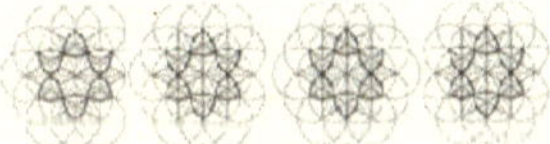

I KNEW the bitter bile of Shiamsa's fear stained brow, her softness cut by witching straps clutched tight in her father's grasp. That was the last time I ever caught a glimpse of her.

The first time we met had been so charmed. I paid a call on David, the burly construction Peace Corps volunteer, in the hopes of straightening out who all the foreigners were in Baidoa. I remember so vividly the shy, sassy smile that peeked around the corner of the kitchen, the eyes that told me I was beautiful too.

I never learned what Shiamsa's nickname was. I am sure she had one. Everyone had a nickname, even

Molly and me. "Molly" and "Moriah" weren't in the Arabic lexicon, so we both got dubbed "Miriam". But they had to tell us apart, so we got nicknames. They called me *"Miriam Yahr"*, "Little Miriam." They called Molly *"Miriam Weyn"*, "Big Miriam". I wore my *"Miriam Yahr"* with pride, even smugness. Molly hated her nickname and tried to convince me it was only because she was older that she was considered "Big." I just nodded knowingly.

Our servant's real name was "Hasan", but we always called him Tifu. "Tifu" meant "skinny", like a twig. Tifu may have been skinny when he was born, but he was a strong man when I met him. Tifu must have swallowed a lot of pride in his thirty-plus years with a nickname like "Tifu", which may explain how he managed to work for two women, a less than honorable position.

I don't know Shiamsa's nickname. She tried to tell me once, but I didn't know the Somali word, and she didn't know how to tell me in English. We agreed that I would just call her Shiamsa. It was such a lovely name, and she was a lovely young woman, probably three or four years younger than my twenty four years. The question "How old are you?" was a non-question in Somalia. Time was simply gauged differently. There was "the time of the big floods" or "the time of the clan gathering", but there were no dates as in our Gregorian calendar.

While each family could trace its heritage back to the Prophet Mohammed, there was woefully little history, written or oral, prior to that. We do know that in ancient times Somalia was a huge exporter of exotic spices and woods, the very finest aromatic frankincense and myrrh, meerschaum, and cattle and crops that were prized in the Mediterranean world.

We know this because in the 15th century b.c., Queen Hatshepsut of Egypt sponsored an expedition to the horn of Africa, modern Somalia, then called the Land of Punt. When the expedition returned to Egypt with boatloads of treasure, the Queen had magnificent murals painted on the walls of her palace in the Valley of the Kings depicting the treasures found, and the brotherly peoples found there, depicting, as Queen Hatshepsut put it, "The kindest and most generous people I have ever met."

Those murals exist to this day. So far the archeologists who have studied these murals have been mostly male, but I am hoping that a woman's educated eye will soon view them and tell us even more about the women of early Somalia. This Land of Punt is likely where the Magi found the frankincense and myrrh to take to the Christ child. This truly was a treasured land.

Early visitors to Somalia were enthralled with the treasures there, and didn't try to inflict their rule on these people. There were small skirmishes, of course, but combat was hand-to-hand with swords and knives, and Somalis with their strength and valor stood their ground.

In the 15th century Portugal was the first of many European nations that wanted to rule Africa, including Somalia, for purely political and economic reasons, introducing firearms and massive massacres that wiped out whole villages in a single day. This treasured land – Somalia -- became a killing ground. By the 20th century, Great Britain, France and Italy had carved up Somalia and claimed it as their own.

Throughout their history, Somalis did not enslave people, so being a servant was a very respectable profession. Shiamsa was a servant like Tifu, but was higher ranking than Tifu. She was David's "boyessa", his housekeeper and cook. David had directed the construction of the four-room schoolhouse that Molly and I taught at, as well as four elementary schools in the district. He had arrived a year before us, and, with a six-foot muscular frame, he was taller and stronger than most of the Somalis he worked with. His physical prowess and strong leadership earned him exceptional respect from those he worked with. There were rumors that Shiamsa was David's whore, although David swore that he never touched her. He readily admitted to hiring other local prostitutes, but not Shiamsa.

Whether Shiamsa was David's mistress or not, she clearly enjoyed a position that servants rarely reach. She actually teased him about how tall he was and about the size of his shirts, and sometimes she even sat and had tea with us when I visited. She indeed struck me as a spunky, sharp young woman, and a very pretty one too. She had the mocha brown complexion and huge black eyes of many Somali women, coupled with a natural grace to her every move.

When I received the invitation from the Peace Corps to go to Somalia, I rushed to the local library and looked up "Somalia" in the encyclopedia. There was one column, and one image, that of a group of young warriors with huge Afro hairstyles, the ones I came to know as the powerful young Rahanweyn warriors. That was it. There were no books at all about Somalia. With just that one encyclopedia entry, I knew that this was a people that I yearned to know. It called to me like the mythical Bali Hai.

I hadn't seen images of Somali women until Peace Corps training, an intensive three-month course held at Columbia University in New York. The images we saw at training had been taken by male staff members, and since it was forbidden by the Moslem religion to have one's image captured on film, the women we saw in those pictures were not the women I met later. The women in these photos were likely sophisticated city women from Mogadishu, and they were posing for a photographer with a western eye, with chins lowered and a demure look. These women were Somali, but they were far more westernized than the women of Baidoa.

The women of Baidoa were much more beautiful, their beauty reflected through their internal strength, with the power of their heads held high above strong backs, with a pride in their stride and steadfast gaze. It was a strength, a power, that affirmed, "Go ahead, make me bear children in pain; I will thrive. Go ahead, take away four out of every five babes that I bear; I will but care for those who survive even more. Go ahead, bring drought to my family; I will find ways to make them live." It was a defiance, an inner strength, a complete trust in Allah that was absolutely uncompromising. Like Steinbeck's women in "The Grapes of Wrath," Somali women were unquestionably the core of the family, hence the core of Somali society, and they wore that responsibility with dignity.

This is not what I expected in a country where young girls were routinely mutilated with clitorectomies. But that is how it was.

Shiamsa was promised in marriage to Abdullahi, a young man in a neighboring town. They had met at a wedding dance in Baidoa about two years previously, and Abdullahi had courted Shiamsa through clandestine meetings at the springs and along paths at the edge of town. Arranged marriages were only slowly being replaced by love matches, so they knew they had to be careful. When they were certain of their love, Abdullahi spoke with his parents who in turn went to speak with Shiamsa's family. Over many meetings and more cups of tea they negotiated the bride price and began exchanging gifts between the families. Abdullahi didn't yet have enough money for the bride price, nor enough to support a family, so Shiamsa was waiting until he was ready, and in the interim they had the joy of seeing each other from time to time.

There were no old maids in Somalia. In a land where a man could have as many as four wives if he could support them, women were in demand, usually through an arrangement made by the girl's parents. That happened with Fatuma, Shiamsa's older sister. When Fatuma was likely in her late teens, word was put out that the family was looking for a good husband for her. An older man in a nearby village came to call, and the marriage was arranged, without Fatuma ever having seen her future husband. Everyone said it was a good marriage, joining two equally strong families, and Shiamsa assured me that Fatuma was indeed very happy in her new life, and had already had their first child.

Our friendship was so serendipitous, the one between Shiamsa and me. Here, in the midst of thorn bush country, I found someone very special. Shiamsa once discovered a small blue flower in a bitter dry season and presented it to me with a shyness that conveyed that she knew how much it meant to me ...

how much she meant to me. I taught Shiamsa how to make a chocolate cake for David with a recipe from my Fannie Farmer cookbook, a staple in any Peace Corps trunk. Shiamsa couldn't read or write, but like all Somalis she had an incredible memory and remembered the whole process with just one showing. We had a tin gasoline can that we had converted into our oven. We placed it over hot coals and piled more hot coals on top, creating an oven-like temperature. I made some spectacular cookies and cakes in that contraption.

Somalis did bake sometimes, in a round clay sort of oven. During the Italian occupation after World War II they learned to bake a kind of small loaf of bread which the Italians ate with the local spaghetti. The bread was hard, and the spaghetti tasteless, but it kept them – and us --alive. Still our tin can was unique. Shiamsa loved learning how to use it, and I had one made especially for her.

Shiamsa taught me how to negotiate with the local merchants, although I never got very good at it. It seemed to me that the prices were so low to begin with that I felt guilty arguing about making them even lower. Shiamsa laughed at me when we went to market. Shiamsa also taught me how to make the aromatic black Arabic tea brewed with lots of sugar and laced with cardamom and cinnamon, something that Tifu would never have shown me. Somalis drank that sticky sweet tea morning and night.

One afternoon Shiamsa and I sat drinking the sweet cardamom tea, alone at my house. The Catholic orphanage where I taught in the afternoons had a holiday that day, Molly was out teaching at the Police station, and Tifu had left for the day.

Shiamsa told me about a cousin who was visiting from the north. No one knew him, but according to Somali custom, he was welcomed. He had spent the last evening telling tales of the merchants in Hargeisa and how the northern Somali nomads were dealing with the heavy rains that year. Shiamsa had obviously practiced this little story so she could tell it to me in perfect English, which she nearly managed to do. Her effort pleased me so.

Shiamsa was wearing a new dress, at least one I hadn't seen before, and I commented on how lovely it was. Yellow flowers libbety-skittered over a bright tangerine background, with bursts of burgundy and evergreen.

"Is that a new dress?" I asked. "It really is pretty."

Shiamsa always wore the traditional draped dress of east African women, most often her rose pink and deep lavender flowered fabric. It was tied on one shoulder, then draped around her twice and tied again in front at the waist, probably three to four yards of fabric altogether. With a bright blue head scarf that covered every wisp of hair, and a gold flowered shawl for cool evenings, Shiamsa always looked very colorful.

Somali women made no attempt at matching the head scarf or shawl, so the whole ensemble was a riot of flowers beyond anything in their own landscape. Even the desert when it bloomed each year for just a few days did not remotely compare to the cacophony of colors in the Somali draped gowns, as if the women's spirits cried out for something beautiful. Whenever we went to the marketplace, the colorful flowered fabrics favored by Somali women, the ones imported from India, Egypt and China, absolutely burst with energy.

Like most Somali women, Shiamsa had very few dresses, wearing each dress for years, often even when it took on the brown tones of Somali soil and eventually fell apart. New fabrics crinkled and folded with a will of their own, but as the fabric became accustomed to a woman's body, it flowed and accented the woman's natural curves. I knew well that Shiamsa's natural curves whispered a fantasy. I knew her every nuance by watching the flow of her dresses.

Today Shiamsa wore the new dress with golds and greens and magentas.

"Yes, it is new," Shiamsa said. "I am happy you like it. You. Me." Her finger moved back and forth between us. I knew she wanted us to switch clothes, and she began to untie the knot at her waist.

"Oh, no," I protested. "I don't even know how."

Shiamsa quickly closed the shutters in the living room, leaving the only light creeping in from the kitchen window. She smiled playfully, so pleased that she could show me something new. She deftly untied the knot at her waist and unwound the fabric from her body, then untied the knot at her shoulder. She stepped out of the length of cloth, leaving the yellow flowers tumbled on the floor. She wore no undergarments. Her deep amber skin played with the shafts of sunlight; her flawless breasts and thighs threw me on a runaway roller coaster ride– light-headed, my gut lurching at the danger as we careened around sharp curves.

Even when Shiamsa draped her gossamer shawl over her shoulder, her beauty only glowed stronger. Her skin glistened in the afternoon heat, from her tiny toes peeking out from a printed hibiscus to her gently rounded tummy and womanly nipples begging for attention. I ached to bury my lips in her softness.

I stood glued to my spot, terrified of what I might do. After months of intolerable isolation in Baidoa, Shiamsa stood naked in front of me, only a few inches away. She and I had never touched, never held hands, or hugged on meeting. That simply was not done. Ever. Part of me wanted to reach for her, and relish every inch of her radiance. Part of me chilled at the danger.

Before I could regain my senses, Shiamsa had unbuttoned the three buttons on my blouse and untied the bow on my loose wrap-around skirt, setting the blouse and skirt gently on the back of the chair.

Shiamsa reached down and gathered up the yellow flowers from the floor. It was an image worthy of Frida Kahlo. Golds and russets and greens tumbled over her arms as she found the fabric corner she was looking for. As she reached to drape the flowered fabric over my shoulder, her hand brushed my breast, ever so softly and, I thought, paused just a fraction of a second.

"Oh my heavens," I thought. "Could she hear my heart screaming?"

I reached for her hand, wanting so desperately to hold it tight to my breast, for just a moment. But a burst of sunlight flooded the room. The front door was shoved wide open, and Tifu stood, outlined by the brilliance of the setting sun.

" **AAAIII !!**"

"**AAAIII !!**"

"**AAAIII !!**"

I'm not sure which of us screamed the loudest – Shiamsa, Tifu or me. Tifu dropped the parcel he was carrying, turned and ran.

I lunged at the door, slamming it shut. There was no locking it. It simply had no lock. I slipped on the broken eggs that Tifu had dropped on the cement floor. By the time I got up, Shiamsa had her own dress back on, and was trying to get my clothes back on me.

"*Bismelahi Bismilahi.*" Shiamsa kept repeating that phrase, or something like it, and some others that I didn't know at all. I was too stunned to say anything.

I didn't realize until much later that Shiamsa wasn't apologizing for anything that might – or might not – have happened between us; I think perhaps that fantasy was mine alone. Although homosexuality was punishable by death according to Sharia law, I wasn't at all certain that the concept applied to women, nor did I have the courage to ask. No, I believe Shiamsa was mortified because a man – a servant – had seen us naked. Shiamsa was a virgin, and being seen by any man, let alone a lowly one, was strictly forbidden in the Moslem tradition. She was stunned. Because Tifu had seen me too, she assumed my reaction was the same, and she was right. Having my male servant catch me at that moment was horrifying enough, but I was terrified too that something truly dreadful would happen to Shiamsa. I didn't know what might happen, but I knew that this was a very unusual experience. I chastised myself for allowing it to happen, and for weeks I couldn't even look at a Somali woman, fearful that their eyes would bore into my innermost thoughts, telling me what a fool I was for harming one of their own. And they were right.

From then on, I made a point of checking with David every few days to reassure myself that Shiamsa was still working for him, and that she was okay.

Shiamsa and I never again shared a cup of tea. I don't think either of us knew how to continue the conversation, and I hadn't a clue how to make it right.

Shiamsa and I did meet again, very unexpectedly, a few months later. Shiamsa darted in front of me as I left the adult night class that I taught in the village. It was dark by then and I nearly collided with her.

"Come," Shiamsa instructed. She turned and headed down the path, over the soccer field area now grown tall with scratchy grasses, the same path I took home every night that I taught school. Here is where school boys played soccer most afternoons, where I had been drafted as a referee although I knew woefully little about soccer. This was my home turf. As we reached the edge of the grassy area Shiamsa put her right hand under her shawl and began almost shouting in Somali. I heard a mumbling from somewhere as the grasses swayed and jumbled.

"What's happening?" I whispered furtively.

"I talk, my knife. I talk, my brothers watch," Shiamsa explained. Pointing to the edge of the field she stated, "My brothers are there, and there."

"Who?" It seemed such an absurd question. "Talk to who?"

"They kill you."

It felt like hours before we reached the far end of the field. Omar Chicago came running out of the compound, obviously frantic. He and Shiamsa exchanged a few brisk sentences, then Shiamsa left with Omar's eldest son beside her. Omar told me to get inside.

"What's going on?" I felt like I missed something.

Omar briskly explained. "Men kill you. Shiamsa take you home."

"But couldn't Shiamsa's brothers have just walked me home?" It seemed so simple to me.

"Brothers in Mogadishu," said Omar.

I went inside, sat and cried, chills running down my spine. I knew there were strong anti-American sentiments in Somalia, in spite of the efforts of President Shermake, the president of Somalia at that time. Shermake's goal was to ease tensions on all fronts, and it was a slow process. I often felt a chill when I went into town, but this was the first time I felt a direct threat. Molly was already asleep when I got home. I closed all the shutters and once again I regretted that the door didn't have a lock. I needn't have worried. When I peeked out the door a few minutes later, Omar's son had returned and was stationed securely in front of our door, a very long knife at his side, held fast by the leather crafted sheath and belt. After that I noticed that often when I walked home at night there was someone – or something -- along the edge of the field, watching. But it wasn't a menacing presence at all. It may have been one of Omar's sons, just keeping me safe, or perhaps

Shiamsa's brothers, or Shiamsa herself. Or perhaps it was the presence of a Goddess I had never met.

LIFE IN BAIDOA returned to normal, if indeed there was such a thing.

Sometimes when I stopped at David's place, I saw Shiamsa's shadow tossed against the kitchen wall. That was as close as I got to her. I wanted so desperately to tell her how grateful I was for her risking her life to save mine, if indeed I could find the words to say so. But she didn't wish to be seen.

I did have one thing that I thought I could safely give her, a slim gold filigree bracelet that I had purchased in Mogadishu shortly after we arrived. I had stumbled upon the old Arabic quarter where goldsmith shops snuggled together in the shadows of narrow alleyways, perhaps a dozen or so shops, one after the other. Here were Arabian goldsmiths who used only 22 karat gold, the very purest gold used in jewelry, creating treasures with techniques perfected over millennia. I watched as they melted the gold, and pulled out threads thin as the strands in a spider's web, then wound the strands around and around creating a delicate lace design in bracelets, brooches and earrings. The pieces were sold by weight, not by intricacy, so I simply picked out a piece I liked, a slim gold filigree bracelet, and had it weighed. It only cost about twenty dollars, and likely would have been less if I had known how to bargain. So I tucked that lovely gold bracelet into my suitcase, knowing I would be able to wear it somewhere. I hadn't worn it at all in Baidoa, so it seemed the ideal gift for Shiamsa.

I asked David if he would give the gold filigree bracelet to Shiamsa for me, and soon after that David left for the States. His two-year tour was up. David told me that he found Shiamsa a very good job with a government family, and that he left her a nice bonus for all her hard work.

I saw her just one more time.

I had wandered into a part of the village that I had never seen before. Each round adobe hut looked identical to me, but the naked children running around seemed to know which one was theirs. Women tended the fires in the courtyards. A few looked up and acknowledged me, most ignored me, simply tossing scraps to chickens and goats, or grinding sorghum into flour with mortar and pestle.

I heard a scream, a low suppressed scream in a woman's voice, like a lamb bleating. Everything stopped. Then I saw a circle of men with a woman, her gold and magenta flowered dress trailing in the dust, dancing in the middle of the circle while the men stomped and clapped. One man wielded a leather strap that he used to lash out at the woman every time she faltered. And I saw a glint of gold on her arm. I knew that woman. Here was the tender, beautiful, loving woman who had saved my life. Welts scarred her arms and legs. I had heard of this barbaric custom. It was a *lumbi* ritual, a brutal custom of the Benadiri tribe, designed to drive out evil spirits from the body of the possessed. I recalled that Shiamsa told me she was of the Benadiri tribe, a tribe centered in Mogadishu, but I was horrified to see her so brutalized.

Shiamsa saw me. Our eyes locked for but an instant, and she pleadingly, gently shook her head "No." Whatever was happening, I couldn't be part of it. I was petrified, afraid that even my presence would make it worse, so I backed away as softly and as rapidly as possible.

When I saw Omar Chicago that afternoon I asked him about Shiamsa.

"What has happened to Shiamsa?" I pleaded for an answer, some acknowledgement that she was okay.

Omar spat on the ground. "Gone" was all he said. He was clearly angry with me, and he clearly did not want to talk about it.

I was bitterly angry with myself. David was gone; he couldn't protect her any more. Nor could I. All I had done was bring her misery.

I was bitterly angry with Tifu too. What had he told people that could have turned them against her so? In truth, it might not have been Tifu who told tales. Perhaps someone visiting Omar's compound saw or heard something. Perhaps Shiamsa herself had said something to someone, although I doubted it. Perhaps it erupted from something totally unrelated to our misadventure. I would never know.

Shiamsa was simply "gone". I searched the sky, hoping beyond hope that she might appear.

I cried out for the Somali Goddess Arawello, for any Goddess who might hear my plea. "Please protect this beautiful young woman. Please."

I needed to talk with someone. Who? Not a single soul came to mind. David was the only one who would understand how very special Shiamsa was, and he too was gone. Bereft of Bibles and Torahs, I took out my slim volume of Emily Dickinson poems. Here I stood beneath the bursting Milky Way reading Emily by starlight, a magical spot where few were blessed to be. I didn't feel blessed at all; I felt cursed, a Cassandra dumping misery on those I loved.

"Hope is the thing with feathers on –
that perches on the soul."

Emily wrote that long ago. I knew that Hope … that Dream … that Chill that wafted o'er me so.

"And sings the tune without the words
And never stops – at all –"

Mohammed and His Donkey

(This story was translated from the Arabic by Fatuma, one of my summer school students at Sheik Awes Middle School. It was first published in "Stories told by Somalis", a collection that Tom and I put together of some of the best work from the summer students ~ Miriam Yahr)

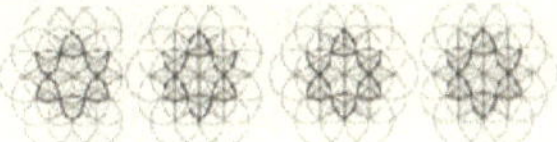

ONE DAY a man named Mohamed put a heavy load on his donkey and went to the town. On the way, the donkey stopped because the load was too heavy. He sat down and refused to go on. Mohamed didn't know what to do.

He saw a friend, Abdurahaman, and asked him to help. Abdurahaman came over and looked at the donkey. He grabbed the tail and pulled and pulled to make him stand up. But, suddenly, the donkey's tail broke. Mohamed was angry and said, Let's go to the police."

They left, and as they were walking, they met a policeman and told him about the donkey. The policeman said, "Let your friend go."

So, they went to Mohamad's house and Mohamed told his wife to give some food to Abdurahaman. Then he left to buy some things in the town.

While the wife was making the food, Abdurahaman wanted some water from the kitchen. When he stood up, he stepped on the baby who was sleeping on the floor and broke its stomach.

The mother cried and cried.

Finally, Mohamed returned and said, "Let's go to the police."

The friend said, "O.K."

As they were walking on the road, Abdurahaman saw a tall tree and hid behind it. When Mohamed reached the station, he looked behind him and didn't see Abdurahaman. He ran towards his house, looking for Abdurahaman, but he didn't find him. Mohamed told his wife what had happened.

Then Abdurahaman said, "What will I do now?"

He climbed a tall tree. An old man was walking near the tree. Abdurahaman wanted to kill himself, and he jumped from the tree. He fell on the shoulders of the old man and killed him.

....

The story of Abdurahaman has haunted me for decades, What do you do with a friend who destroys so much?

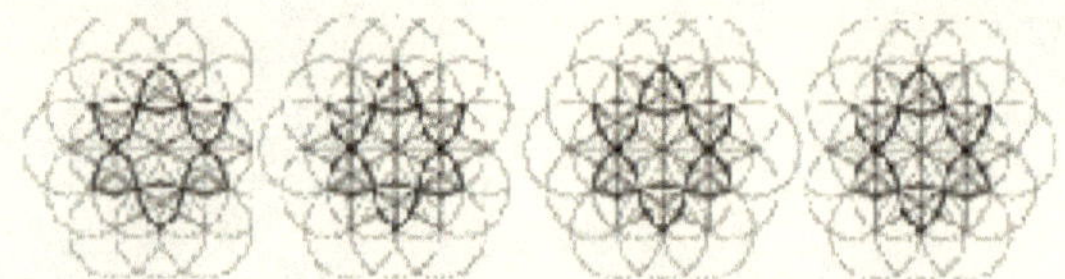

Ali Ahmed in Sharp Shooter Alley

*And when the din of the battle resounds all
around
On that day is not he who fights bravely
like a lion attacking?
(from "The Path of Righteousness" by Mahammed
Abdille Hasan)*

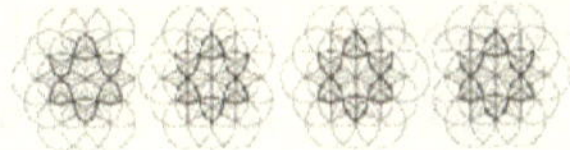

THEY ROARED, they cheered, that crowd of two hundred. Women's gay dresses billowed in the breeze, while men bartered vociferously, arms waving, challenges being tossed like trading cards, while children scampered around legs and skirts. It felt like a festival. Everyone had gathered along

Sharp Shooter Alley, that dirt patch on the outskirts of Baidoa, for one reason: To determine the greatest archer in the Upper Juba region.

The crowd hushed for a moment, then flew into wild raging shouts as Ali Ahmed, the acclaimed local top archer, stepped out from behind the seven-foot tall target at the end of the crowded alleyway. Ali Ahmed was not seven foot tall. In fact, he was rather diminutive, perhaps barely grazing five foot tall, but his grin likely stretched all of seven feet all by itself. Ali Ahmed, an older man by any measure, probably in his fifties, stood grinning, nearly toothless, with his once-white cotton shirt and once-red plaid wrap around. He held his right hand high, holding his bow for all to see. This was the bow constructed from a local scraggly tree, and it had served him well as challenger after challenger confronted him. His left hand deftly guided his wooden crutch as he placed his wooden leg with practiced skill.

Ali Ahmed took his time walking down the alley. Male town folk, young Rahanweyn warriors with their immaculate huge hair styles, and nomads of all ilk stepped forward to shake his hand, and he accepted each hand with grace. Molly and I, and all the ex-pats and foreigners for miles around, stood in awe of this man, tipping our hats or nodding. He was clearly a champion.

When Ali Ahmed reached the spot for the archers, he unhooked his peg leg, put it on the ground and sat on it, all the while grinning from ear to ear. He was ready for the next challenger.

Today Ali Ahmed was facing a challenger like none other.

… And there he was, a six-foot tall man in his late fifties, in the prime of his life. A white man. This was Conn Price, the junior scientist at the USAID station on the far side of Baidoa. Conn and his wife Sallie were a special couple. They had adopted Molly and me, taking us to an Eid celebration, the grand party culminating a month of fasting for Ramadan, where we sang and danced into the night. They took us on a camping trip to the local airstrip, where we woke to a circle of young Rahanwen warriors staring down at us. Conn playfully grinned and offered the warriors a cup of coffee, which they declined, and laughing, they disappeared into the bush. Conn and Sallie were just fun people.

When Conn learned of the prowess of the local archer, he could not resist. He had to challenge Ali Ahmed. A date was set, and here we all were. As Conn walked down Shooter Alley, he held his bow above his head, an Olympic-worthy bow made of the finest wood. He waved to the crowd too, but they didn't come forward to shake his hand, they simply stood in awe of that bow, a cobweb of murmurs springing from side to side.

Conn leaned to shake Ali Ahmed's hand, and held out his stylish bow for Ali Ahmed to admire, which Ali Ahmed certainly did. Ali Ahmed offered his bow to Conn as well, and each admired the other's equipment. But this challenge was more than a battle of equipment; it was a battle of skill and determination.

There were to be twenty arrows each, alternating archers. The one with the most arrows in the bull's eye would win. Conn graciously insisted that Ali Ahmed go first. Ali Ahmed chose his arrow, raised his bow to chest height, and let it fly. The arrow hit the target, but not the bull's eye. No matter … everyone cheered and whooped and clapped, including me. I loved this old guy. Ali Ahmed's grin was infectious, and the joy that he generated in this crowd was simply astonishing. Then Conn let fly with an arrow, and it came about three inches closer to the bull's eye. Everyone cheered, but not with the enthusiasm that echoed for Ali Ahmed. And so the match continued. Ali Ahmed shot his arrow, and Conn shot his just a bit better, sometimes hitting the bull's eye. After every round a young lad ran out and pulled the arrows from the target, returning them to their respective owners.

Somewhere around the fifth or sixth round, Ali Ahmed actually beat Conn, hitting the bull's eye straight on. The crowd went nuts. I did too. One of the agriculture Peace Corps volunteers sidled over to me.

"Why are you cheering so loud?" he asked, grinning. "Don't you know that you are the prize for the winner?"

"The whaaaaaat?" I was astounded. Angry. Confused. And really ticked off. I was probably the only one in the crowd who didn't know that I was designated to be the spoils of the battle. That had to be Conn's idea of a joke.

My lesbian nature kicked in. I didn't want to get stuck with any man, and certainly not Conn Price or Ali Ahmed. The notion revolted me.

My feminist nature kicked in too. What right did any man, even Conn Price, have to treat me like some camel, and possess me at all? What right did Conn Price have to name himself tribal chief and give his women away? Sure, Conn was likely to win the match, but what if he didn't? Just what if he didn't? What was he going to do then? The fact that it was just plain wrong to endorse Somalis' view of women as chattel likely didn't even enter Conn's mind. He could have offered some prime sorghum seed, or lent out the USAID tractor for a day, or offered a goat for a feast. He had lots of options, he didn't have to put me up as the prize.

I felt like vomiting.

I slowly slipped out of the crowd and made my way home, hiding behind bushes so no one would see me leave. Actually, I doubt that anyone even noticed that I left. Here I was trying so hard to hold onto what drop of dignity I still had, to find my way back to making a real contribution to Baidoa, and all that my countrymen could do was treat me like a piece of meat, like a joke. My face burned as if someone had slapped me.

I had to wonder too if my lesbianism was the worst kept secret in Baidoa. Did Conn and Sallie know? Did the other Peace Corps volunteers know? For certain, they knew I was somehow different. I was different. I walked a thin line between being interested in them personally while not encouraging any romantic interest. Most of the time I feared that I failed miserably and just came across as, well … weird. That was the word that one of the agriculture volunteers used one night when he didn't know I could hear him. "Yeah," he said, "Molly is okay. But Moriah is just weird."

I wished I could have spoken with Conn Price and just told him why his "joke" troubled me so, but that just wasn't an option.

So I slipped through the shadows of the thorn bushes, slowly making my way home. Alone.

Another Glass of Wine

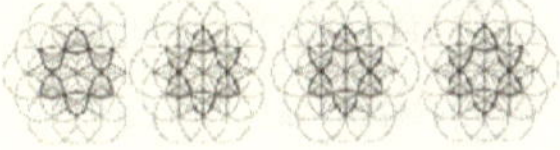

I SAT IN Luigi's compound while Luigi poured what was at least the second glass of wine for me. It may have been my third, or my fourth, truly I didn't know. Luigi never offered Molly or me a second glass of wine. He rarely even invited us to his compound, leaving our pounding on his gate unanswered.

But I was inside the compound, sitting at a small table with Luigi. No one else was there. I didn't even know how I had gotten there. *Perhaps*, I thought, *I have slipped across time into a comfortable dimension.* Luigi, the old Italian curmudgeon with the wine cellar, sat patiently. I clutched his handkerchief and every so often I rather inelegantly blew my nose.

"She was so beautiful," I told Luigi. "And I destroyed her life."

Luigi held his hand to his heart and pointed at me quizzically. A matter of the heart? He was Italian, he knew all about matters of the heart. I nodded.

"She was going to be married, and I ruined that. I've ruined so much. And I was going to change the world, or at least my corner of it. Well, I changed it all right. Maybe I'll rot in hell, and it would serve me right. That's what an *iman* told me a few days ago. He said America was lying about flying around the earth, that the Koran said the earth was flat, so it was flat. America said the earth was round, and all of us liars and infidels would burn in hell." I paused to blow my nose and get a good gulp of wine. Luigi's wine was several rungs better than the rot gut in Mogadishu and I felt guilty enjoying it.

"Willow, my lover back home, had the good sense to dump me. River told me so in her letter. And River told me about a singer they all saw at the Monterey Jazz Festival, someone named Janis Joplin. Do you know her? No, I don't either. And this other one … Chris Williams. He sings about changing. Maybe they will be in Woodstock in the summer – River says I have to go. Heck, I don't even know where Woodstock is. I feel like there's a huge world out there somewhere, changing, and I'm here in this cramped cave, surrounded by man-eating thorn bushes and suffocating in rain and red dust.

"River said I'm really missing a lot by not being there – the marches in San Francisco, the demonstrations. She said they are changing the world. Drat it, I could have changed the world from home, I didn't have to come here. Here all I've done is jump from misery to blunder to disaster," and I jumped my now empty wine glass around the red squares on the checkered table cloth.

"They killed Martin Luther King," I said softly. "I should be at home."

Luigi spoke no English, and I spoke no Italian, but the kindness in his sitting there with me touched me deeply. He started to refill my glass once more, but I said no. I wasn't entirely sure I could walk home as it was. As I stood to leave, he wrapped me in a shawl, protection against the evening chill, and walked beside me all the way home.

As we reached Omar Chicago's gate, I put my fingers to my lips, then touched his cheek. "*Grazie, Luigi.*"

Luigi smiled a gentle smile. "*Ciao, mia piccola amica.*"

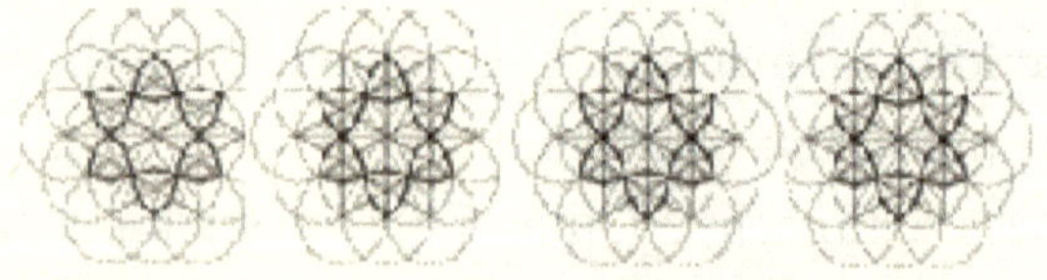

Full Circle Mosaic

*"Many sheep and goats, cattle and camels: all the
riches of the world "*
(Somali saying)

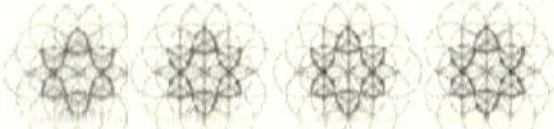

June 1968

HERE I WAS AGAIN, right where I had started just
a month earlier. This was my quiet place, my
private space, this stretch of seaside along the
Indian Ocean in Mogadishu. Here is where I
opened to ocean breezes, let them infuse me with
their regenerative spirit. I grew up along the Pacific
Coast, dancing to the myriad moods of the wild
ocean. Living in Baidoa was the first time in my life

that I could not go to the seashore anytime I wished, and I treasured these moments so. The Indian Ocean was much calmer, a balm to my sometimes restless moods.

As soon as summer school at Sheik Awes School in Baidoa had ended, I headed to Mogadishu to begin my own vacation, roughly four weeks of doing anything that I wanted to do.

I spotted Julia, the beautiful Peace Corps volunteer stationed in Kismayo, on the coast south of Mogadishu. I had become intrigued with Julia during Peace Corps training in New York. It was impossible to miss her – she was the one with a coterie of admirers bustling about. Her soft auburn curls skipped in the breeze on the verandah where we had coffee each morning, her broad smile greeting me. I wanted to believe that her smile was just for me, but she smiled at everyone, and everyone smiled back. She held court for her admirers every morning on that verandah. I joined that table from time to time, but I was only a shadow sitting there. Everyone but Julia ignored me, and Julia never failed to compliment me on a pretty scarf, or ask my opinion on the subject at hand. She cared for her adoring subjects well.

When I saw Julia in Mogadishu, she was uncharacteristically alone, sitting on the stone fence edging the ocean. We immediately fell into a reverie about all the wonderful places we wanted to go on vacation. All the Peace Corps volunteers had the month of June off, free to do as we wished. This was the main reason I joined the Peace Corps in the first place: to see exotic spots in the world that I would never see otherwise. Being a "do-gooder" was a nice idea, but being a traveler to faraway places was even better. I definitely counted Baidoa as an "exotic spot", and here was my chance to visit even more. Some Peace Corps volunteers were going to Egypt or India, but Julia and I wanted to tour East Africa, all around Lake Victoria.

"I'd love to see Lake Victoria," I said.

"Yes!" said Julia, "and take an overnight ferry ride."

"… and see live crocodiles and rhinoceroseros …."

"… and Mount Kilimanjaro …"

"… They say Kilimanjaro is so magical. And Zanzibar!"

"… Yes, Zanzibar, with all its exotic spices, and Parra Lodge …"

"… where the monkeys and elephants come to play each evening …"

We laughed as we completed each other's thoughts on all the incredible treasures we could see.

"Would you travel with me?" That was Julia speaking, and I could hardly believe it. She spoke as though I would be doing her a favor by travelling with her.

Ohmygoodness, would I like the Wizard of Oz to grant my most private wish? A whole month traveling around East Africa with this tantalizing creature? Oh, yes!

We decided to waste no time. We would leave that very afternoon.

And so our adventure began.

WE HEADED FOR KISMAYO, so Julia could show me some of her town. We traveled across the equator, toasting the world with tepid beer along with several dozen other travelers.

We had two days before our plane would arrive to whisk us off to Mombasa, our first stop, and we made the best of every moment. We saw the merry monkeys swinging over the bridge that crossed the Juba River. Julia took off her bright blue head scarf, playing with one of the monkeys who absconded with it, and swinging up to the highest rung of the bridge, sat laughing at us. That was ok. We laughed too.

We took a leaky, muddy ferry over the Juba River to a small island where one Peace Corps volunteer had developed an experimental farm. Although we arrived dirty and disheveled, we were treated royally by the local governor, spending the night in the government guest house. We were even served fresh coconut milk still in coconuts, along with mountains of papaya, mangos and bananas, a treat I could never have tasted in Baidoa. The governor told us to put our shoes and dirty clothes outside our door at night and – voila! – in the morning everything was crispy clean.

On our return back over the Juba River we rode in a squeaky clean ferry – it was the same ferry as before, but it was cleaned up in our honor! It wouldn't have been half as much fun if Julia hadn't slipped and fallen head over tin cups into the muck just before we boarded. She laughed as loudly as any of the villagers, endearing herself to them, and to me.

We took afternoon tea at a banana plantation, and visited a cotton gin run by a Greek born in Egypt who delighted in speaking French with us. Julia promised to bring him some cigars from Kenya.

We had lunch of Scandinavian delicacies aboard a Danish ship docked in the Kismayo harbor that was loading bananas headed for Italy, and we invited a dozen crew members to an impromptu party at the home of a USAID secretary that Julia knew, dancing far into the wee hours of the next morning.

Like two anxious travelers, we packed our bags early the next morning and headed out to the tiny Kismayo airport, ready to catch our flight to Mombasa to begin our "real" vacation. Our "bags" were actually two large woven sisal baskets, one for Julia and one for me. We thought those baskets would be easier to handle than suit cases, something we could keep close at hand.

Sadly our scheduled Somali Air flight declined to stop for us. We saw it approaching, a bit high it seemed, and it just flew over. The ticket master told us the pilot was told by Mogadishu that the Kismayo Airport was flooded, and so wouldn't stop. Julia and I simply looked at each other, distraught. We were standing on solid ground. There was no flooding.

As fate would have it, we were offered a chartered plane to Nairobi at no charge. It didn't matter to us whether we began our journey in Mombasa or in Nairobi, we simply wanted to begin. The USAID couple who chartered the flight from Nairobi to Kismayo was returning from vacation, and the four-seater prop plane was scheduled to return to Nairobi empty, so we were thrilled to accept the invitation.

ALONG OUR TRULY awe-inspiring journey around Lake Victoria we felt the thunder of Murchinson Falls, the 150 foot drop between the White Nile and Lake Victoria, the gorge being only seven meters wide, the falls crashing so loudly that it shoved out any feelings I had at all – good or bad – and left me empty, fresh for new beginnings. I reached for Julia's hand as we stood there, as if to assure myself that the world still existed.

We stood in respectful amazement, watching the sea of pink flamingos at Lake Nakuru.

We embraced the reverent silence that overtook the passengers on the train as we sped across the valley, watching Mount Kilimanjaro come into view. Even the children knew that something was different here, as if the spirit of Kilimanjaro reached out to embrace us. I was closest to the window looking toward Mount Kilimanjaro. Two Ugandan children came over to our window, the little girl sitting on my lap, and the little boy scrunched against the car siding. Julia rested her arm across the seat and leaned into me to get a good view. It was a lovely moment -an impromptu family.

We treasured the beautiful smile of the small girl in Kisumu who picked a wild poinsettia and gave it to me when she saw that I admired it. She picked another for Julia when Julia came to see my poinsettia, then she ran off smiling and laughing.

We felt the serenity of the truce that the wild creatures of Parra Lodge declare each evening at dusk so that each in turn can drink at the best water hole. Lions and wild pigs, hippos and elephants, giraffes and all the other creatures really do live at peace, each taking its turn to drink. There was no need for these creatures to kill each other, for they each had enough food and water every single day. We had dinner that evening with a couple from India who taught us the joy of eating spicy hot Indian curries.

Our entire trip was surrounded by more than "lush" vegetation. We sought treks via back roads on busses and trains, along the way watching the tiny villages peek out from behind massive bushes, with bougainvillea pinks and poinsettia reds framing every moment. Tall palm trees, jungle trees with huge elephant ears, and vines in all shades of vermillion, sapphire and rust sprang from every inch, hugging small villages of round mud huts with pointed thatched roofs. Children waved at our train wherever we were, and there were smiling people at every stop selling local baked cassava, fresh papayas and coconuts, and freshly cooked meat on long skewers. No matter whether we were on a train, a bus, or an eight-seater van, we encountered nothing but smiles.

Julia was a master at making friends on our journey. Once Julia helped a young boy, about twelve years old, care for his five siblings on the bus while his mother went to get them dinner, and when their mother returned with dinner, she had dinner for Julia and me too.

A group of children in Mwanza showed us shops owned by their mothers and fathers where we purchased brilliant jewel-tone lengths of fabric – Julia's soft rippling laughter had shopkeepers searching through huge piles of fabric to find just the perfect selections for us, a lively tangerine and lemon design for Julia, and a vibrant emerald and gold design for me.

We gladly accepted the help of a young college student, a student nurse, who helped us decipher a menu in Tanga, providing us a dinner of savory goat rather than questionable monkey meat.

We will be forever grateful to the ship's captain of the ferry on Lake Victoria -- our dream "cruise" had rammed into a tropical storm, and with both of us frantically trying to keep our stomachs intact, this incredibly gracious captain invited us up from second class to join the diners in first class where we could get some soup and tea.

FINALLY, WE ANXIOUSLY approached the mysteries of Zanzibar.

This was one of the spots highest on our "to visit" list, and the main reason we originally wanted to begin our vacation along the Indian Ocean coastline. We flew from Dar es Salaam to Zanzibar, one of only several small planes to take that same route that morning. As we landed in Zanzibar, about a dozen planes were already lined up and unloading passengers, some from as far away as Mombasa and even Nairobi. A small army of local guides lined up to greet us, each clutching a stack of written recommendations from previous clients. We hooked up with a friendly local chap who drove a spiffy clean car. It was my birthday! We were ready for adventure, and our guide did not disappoint.

Our Zanzibar guide drove us through fields of cloves and cinnamon and took us to the huge outdoor market with brilliant orange and yellow umbrellas with coconuts, pineapples, dates, papayas and all manner of exotic fruit. He walked us through tiny alleyways that were built centuries before, with majestic doorways snuggled into corners, all the while telling us the history of this mysterious place. He even showed us an old sultan's palace at the end of a squiggly footpath in a tangled forest, now resting in ruins with overgrown ivies and exotic ferns nearly covering it completely. He pointed out the ancient baths where the sultan's 89 wives bathed. The baths were made of large stones cracked and chipped over the centuries, probably thirty or forty square yards of once luxurious pleasure. With all of the tourists on Zanzibar that day, we were the only ones at the sultan's palace.

We thanked our Zanzibar guide profusely, and tipped him equally well, then opted to head out on our own. First we each purchased an elegant jewelry box covered in intricately molded silver at a shop that our guide had pointed out. Then we headed to the main tourist area in Stone Town, the largest town in Zanzibar.

That is when tears overcame me as we stood on the site of the former slave market in Zanzibar. Tens of thousands of African slaves were processed through this slave market that lasted more than a thousand years supporting the Near East slavery route. An Anglican cathedral has been built on the site now, as if hiding the true significance of this slave market. But all the acres and acres of sweet spices, the cinnamon, cloves, and nutmeg that infuse Zanzibar with mystery cannot wipe out the stench of the past. The guide books say that this elaborately carved cathedral honors the Black lives that passed through here.

No, that is a rotten lie.

No, had the White Man wanted to honor Black slaves, he would have built a monument to African tradition, to honor the millennia of African art, music and philosophy that was lost forever. But here was a huge white Anglican cathedral. Here was a huge monument to White tradition, to the White god who gave his permission for trading in Black flesh.

I watched a young family, a Black man and wife with their two young sons, perhaps eight and twelve years old. The older boy had an American flag and a Boy Scout patch on his backpack, leading me to suspect that they were American tourists too. The older boy was reading from the tourist guidebook to his little brother, and the younger boy's eyes grew wider and wider, as though this was the first time he had truly encountered Black slavery. The older boy took the hand of his younger brother, wanting to lead him into the church. But the younger brother would have none of it – he resisted. He simply would not go.

I didn't want to go inside that church either.

I stepped aside, away from the church and the little historical plaques that had been placed there, away from the respectful smiling tourists, into the silence. And there I heard the cries of the shackled slaves from the soggy rat infested dungeons. Julia was raised in the South and knew well the agony of the slave trade. We couldn't even speak. We stood side by side, in silence.

A FEW DAYS earlier we had gotten a hint of an oddly similar frightening silence. Julia and I had hired a car to take us to visit a Pygmy village, and on the return the driver stopped at the edge of the Congo jungle. Our guide cautioned us to keep him in sight as he led us about twenty yards into the jungle, the dark deep heart of Africa. In those twenty yards the noon day sun had totally disappeared, a victim of vegetation so thick that it is hard to imagine how anything ever grew there in the first place. Near total darkness engulfed us, darkness deeper than a stormy cloud covered midnight, a heavy dark, with eerie swishing in the undergrowth and high-pitched animal cries from above. In spite of the strange animal cries, it was the pervading silence that frightened me.

We stretched our necks, searching for some sunlight to find our direction. But there was no light, there was no way out.

I could barely make out the leaf brushing against my sleeve. When we looked around, our guide was gone. We called, but there was no answer. We grabbed each other's hands in panic, not knowing which way to turn, which way to go to get out, and dreadfully afraid of losing each other. We had lost our guide, and only darkness and bizarre sounds pressed themselves upon us.

Thankfully, just then our guide emerged from behind the bush beside me. "Now you know 'dark'," he said. He was right. Those few moments of fear were all that I wanted of the silence of the dark.

RETURNING TO Dar es Salaam from Zanzibar that evening, Julia and I opted to treat ourselves to the finest meal in all of Dar es Salaam in honor of my birthday. I was twenty-five, a quarter of a century old, and I definitely felt older and wiser than when we began our journey. Our hotel clerk directed us to the Palm Beach Hotel, the largest, and most luxurious hotel in all of Tanzania. We didn't have any dressy clothes, having packed only what would fit into our modest baskets, so Julia loaned me a gorgeous emerald scarf to brighten up my tee shirt and wraparound skirt, and she wore the matching earrings.

The lobster dinner at the Palm Beach Hotel was outstanding, but that was just the beginning. As we sipped our après-dinner coffee, the head waiter approached us, asking if we would like to join the table in the center of the room. We looked over. That table was filled with about a dozen very well dressed middle aged African men, the table positioned to draw attention to itself. A few of the men wore light weight western style suits and ties, several had Nehru style jackets, and some flaunted the African style embellished long boxy shirt over matching pants.

They were clearly top echelon, probably business people or government officials.

"Thank you," I said as nicely as I could, "but no. We will have our coffee here."

The waiter left, delivered our message, then returned, a bit flustered. "They really would like you to join them for coffee," he said.

Again I said No, simply but sternly. Julia and I looked at each other and decided we should have our coffees elsewhere. Then a woman stood up from that table in the center of the room. We hadn't seen her because she was on the far side of the table. She was a majestic African with a blue and gold African style sarong skirt and tailored mid-sleeve jacket that had a commanding matching headdress, sporting what looked to be a solid gold brooch in front, about three inches in diameter. She walked toward us, ants and elephants alike stepping aside for her.

She stopped beside our table, looking down at us, her back straight and proud. "Please do join us," she said. "I am Lucy Ngwale, the Minister of Education. I am dining with other government authorities. I understand that you are Peace Corps volunteers. We would be honored if you joined us for coffee." Her English was clipped British, and impeccable.

I didn't even look at Julia. "Of course," I said. "We too would be honored." We walked behind her as the others made space for us at the table.

Lucy introduced Julia and me to a bevy of ministers, assistant ministers and directors of different agencies, and even the Sudanese ambassador to Tanzania. They were all incredibly gracious, especially when they learned it was my birthday. A large silver coffee urn appeared, and they toasted to my health. I felt very honored.

And the conversations that evening – brisk, witty, insightful, and always respectful.

"Does America have women Ministers?" Lucy knew the answer to that one before she asked it.

"Yes," I said, "but not very many. Women the caliber of Eleanor Roosevelt and yourself are rare in any country." I don't know if she actually knew who Eleanor Roosevelt was, but Lucy knew I was complimenting her, and she smiled in acknowledgement.

Lucy was vocal in her belief that America was producing too many know-nothing college graduates who, she said, didn't want to know anything. She was just as critical of those soft Tanzanian students who wanted everything on a silver platter. Lucy grew up under colonialism, was accustomed to being spat on without even knowing why. That she reached the position of authority that she held spoke volumes of the progress that Africa has made to wipe out colonialism.

"Why does America have such difficulty accepting African sovereignty?" the Minister of Health asked.

"Truly, sir, I don't know," I responded. "I do hope that we in the Peace Corps will take back a new message to the United States, but there are just so few of us." The Minister nodded. He understood the complexity of the issue well.

"Do you believe you are accomplishing anything in Somalia?" That question came from the Assistant Minister of the Interior, a short man with strong eyes that challenged all who dared to look too long.

"Somalia wants to make English the language of the government so that it can function in the modern world of nations. Soon they will speak English as well as you, and that will aid them tremendously. We also have Peace Corps Volunteers building schools and teaching modern agriculture. It is not enough. But it is a beginning. Every task, no matter how immense, needs a beginning"

"What have you learned from being in Africa?" This question came from the Minister of Justice, a tall man in a dark blue European style suit.

"All in all, sir, I think I have personally learned a great deal," I told him. "I understand Somali culture so much better than before I came." I smiled a sad smile as I said, "Before I came I didn't even know

Somalia existed." I think the Minister appreciated the honesty of that statement.

I continued. "And now I have a greater appreciation for the tribal system. I respect the Moslem way of life with its immense spirit of cooperation and unquestioned hospitality. And now that I've seen a bit of East Africa, I am in total wonder of the magnificence of Lake Victoria and Mt. Kilimanjaro and all of the amazing peoples we have met. And when I stood in the slave market area of Zanzibar, I felt so deeply sad." I paused to regain my composure.

"Is American justice better than African justice?" interjected the Minister of Justice.

"I don't know much about African justice," I told the Minister, "but I am certain that a system that evolved over centuries of experience must meet the goals of Africans better than an imported system, a system foisted on them by foreigners." I don't think the Minister expected that response, but he nodded in agreement.

The Minister of Defense idly stirred his coffee. He looked deeply into my eyes. "Don't you think you are being very naïve?" He asked. His question stung. Of course he was right.

"Of course it is naïve," said the Minister of Justice. "It is also very true. How often have we let foreign interference dictate our institutions? Too many times, I think. Far too many times."

For a moment a flash of ideological tension burst in, and I turned to Lucy. "Can you tell me about a few education and welfare projects in Tanzania, and how the evolving world political situation has influenced you?"

Lucy told of dozens of projects, hardly taking a breath. She noted that many of these projects reflected foreign influences, but many grew from Tanzanian culture itself.

I asked the Minister of Defense which country he would most like to be aligned with.

He smiled slyly, and raising an eyebrow said, "All of them." Then he asked me, "Which of your enemies would you most like to toss into space?"

I smiled slyly and said, "All of therm." He roared in appreciation.

We talked until nearly midnight. As it grew late, I told them I had one final question: What would they like me to convey to Americans, should I get the chance to do so?

"Tell them we are ready to meet the world," said Lucy.

"I will," I promised.

As I stood to leave, Lucy touched my hand. "I am sorry for the death of Mr. Kennedy," she said sincerely.

"Thank you," I said. "President Kennedy will be remembered as a great President."

"No,' Lucy protested. "Not President Kennedy. His brother, Bobby Kennedy."

"Bobby Kennedy?" I was surprised. "Did he die?"

"He was assassinated," explained Lucy. "It was about three weeks ago, while he was running to become President."

I sat down, stunned, like someone punched me in the gut. First President Kennedy, then Martin Luther King, Jr., then Bobby Kennedy. Only the echo of their voices remained. "I didn't know," I said. "We haven't seen a newspaper since we left Mogadishu."

The irony escaped none of us. Here I was in the midst of what many considered to be a barbaric country, and my own people were killing our leaders. Julia and I thanked Lucy for her concern, and left somberly.

I woke early the next morning, ready to greet our next adventure, needing to affirm Life. Julia teased me about how I jumped out of bed in the morning. Loose threads of her auburn hair played with the sunlight beginning its day. She was beautiful. If I was the scrappy tabby kitty ready to jump into the next mud puddle, she was the luxurious Persian kitten stretching out in the sunshine. I regretted that our sexual preferences were so different. Julia was dating a USAID guy, expecting him to propose at any time, an invitation she would gladly accept. I respected her wishes and kept my distance ... except for once. Once

– on this morning -- I did kiss her, very softly, while she slept. Her lips were every bit as soft and every bit as sweet as they looked.

I wasn't sure that Julia knew what "lesbian" even meant. Julia had lived a very sheltered life as a southern belle, even bringing her twirling baton to Kismayo with her. Actually, she told me that the Peace Corps brass in New York told her to bring her baton, but the Why of it escaped both of us – the silly thing had no practical use at all in Somalia.

I once told Julia about two women I knew who made a commitment to live their lives together. "Why would they do that?" Julia asked. "Couldn't they find husbands?" Julia truly did not have a clue. As much as I yearned to hold her and tell her how beautiful she was, it just wasn't meant to be. Julia would wed her USAID sweetheart and live happily ever after.

Julia stretched out now, slowly opening one eye, then the other, softly batting her eyelashes as she was wont to do. It never ceased to amaze me how Julia's eyelashes could whip men to their knees. Those eyelashes had gotten us first class treatment on the Lake Victoria cruise, special treats in restaurants and even train passage when all the seats were sold. I doubt that Julia had any idea what she was doing, it just came naturally to her.

"You were very quiet last night," I noted. "Didn't you enjoy the party?"

"Oh, I did enjoy it," she protested. "Mostly I enjoyed watching you spar with a table full of men."

It was surprising how similarly Julia and I viewed men. Early in our trip we hooked up with two Peace Corps guys, "for safety." We dumped them soon after, as soon as we discovered that they wanted to sprint from town to town, checking off locations like a shopping list. Julia and I savored each spot that we visited, each step we took was a new piece in the unique mosaic that was East Africa.

The "safety" issue was a valid one. No one in the world knew where we were. Cell phones had not yet been invented, and we didn't call in to report to anyone -- good grief, we were adults. Peace Corps Somalia didn't ask for an itinerary, and if they had asked for one, we couldn't have given it to them. We rationalized that if anything happened we could contact the American Embassy, or perhaps the local Peace Corps office.

Only once did we regret that we were so alone.

WE HAD RETURNED from dinner in Mombasa. Our hotel had been recommended by our taxi driver that afternoon, so although it was shabby, and it had a few quirks, we opted to spend the night there. One of the quirks was that the bathroom was down the hall, and the bathroom door didn't lock at all. When we arrived, we took turns guarding the bathroom door for each other.

The other, more serious, quirk was that the sleeping room could only be locked and unlocked from the outside. Once inside the room, we couldn't lock the door at all. We fixed that by pushing one of the beds up against the door, believing we were protected.

When we got home from dinner that night, we discovered a third quirk: the noise from the dance hall below was so deafening that we couldn't hear each other shout.

When we tried to leave the room, we discovered our door had been locked, from the outside. We were trapped. We screamed ourselves hoarse, pleading for help, but no help came.

We were on the second floor, so we couldn't just step outside the window. We ended up snaking down a shaky trellis and running to safety in a much bigger, more modern hotel.

The pounding on our hotel room door the next morning, around six o'clock, came from police officers ready to arrest us for leaving the first hotel without paying. For a while we thought we were going to be tossed into jail, but as with most third world countries, a bit of *bakshish* (bribery) spread around gave us our freedom. We figured that the only reason the taxi driver had recommended that shabby hotel in the first place was because his brother owned it.

I couldn't tell you what Mombasa was like. We didn't stay to see it.

I GOT ANOTHER civics lesson in Nairobi as I stood before a Kenyan judge in long black British robes and British white wig, presiding in a very British courtroom.

This time I was on the other side of the law. My wallet had been snitched when Julia and I were shopping, spending the last of our money buying treasures to ship home to America. We were buying Kenyan fabrics with geometric mandala-inspired designs, mahogany boxes carved in relief and ebony statuettes of lions and local tribespeople. True to her promise, Julia found some cigars for her Greek friend in Kismayo.

Suddenly a police officer shouted, "Stop!" and grabbed a well-dressed man nearby, holding up a wallet with a red feather in it. It was my wallet. The police officer immediately apprehended the pick pocket, but I had to go to court the next morning to retrieve my wallet. In this court, the judge wrote down the proceedings in long hand, so it was slow going.

Mercifully, the judge was sympathetic to my plight and only asked me two questions: How did I know the wallet was mine, and How much money was in it? He meticulously wrote out my answers in long hand. The thief got ten lashes since this wasn't his first offense, and I got my wallet back, all the money intact.

MUCH TOO SOON Julia and I stood once again on the Mogadishu shore, neither of us wanting the holiday to end.

"What did you like the best?" Julia asked me.

I paused. "The parts that weren't in the guide book," I answered, "like my amazing birthday dinner."

"Me too," said Julia. "But mostly I am just so glad that you and I traveled together. It would have been so lonely if I had gone by myself."

"Julia, is that you?" A perky little blond lady broke into our conversation. She looked to be about eighteen years old, but was probably older. She exuded the wide-eyed anticipation of a new Peace Corps volunteer. "I saw your picture in the Peace Corps office, and now I bump into you – what a surprise!"

"Yes, I am Julia."

"I am Lori; your new teacher in Kismayo," said the little blond person. "I am so glad I ran across you. I have a million questions. The Peace Corps has a Land Rover ready to take me to Kismayo – are you coming too? Do you have a house there? What is the school like?"

This Lori person kept blabbering on. What in heaven's name was she doing there? What right did she have intruding on our private conversation? Why was Julia tolerating her?

"Excuse me," I said. "It sounds like you two have a lot to talk about. I better go find a ride home myself." I turned to leave. I hadn't taken more than three steps when Julia ran after me.

"I really meant what I said," said Julia as she put her hand on my arm. "Thank you for coming with me."

I held both of her hands, afraid to hold on too tightly. "I am the one who should be thanking you," I said. "Of all the people in the world, there is no one I would rather travel with than you. I know that sounds trite. Dorky even. But it is true. I will miss you."

We hugged for what seemed but a brisk moment, then parted. Julia went back to answer Lori's million questions, and I went to find a van going to Baidoa.

I knew that I wouldn't be able to tell anyone in Baidoa about this incredible vacation, for I knew that few Somalis would ever experience anything akin to what I experienced. Even if they could go to some of the places that I went to, they would go as native Africans, not as American outsiders, and that is a very different experience. Also, I didn't want to appear a braggart, for in truth they had experienced things I would never glimpse.

THE NEXT DAY, July 1st, was the Independence Day celebration in Baidoa. Speeches were spoken, songs were sung, dances were danced. Joy absolutely engulfed the town.

After the formal celebrations, I wandered the town and caught a glimpse of my summer school girls, laughing and running through the crowd. I had first heard their laughter during summer school when I had asked each girl to be a Teacher for a Day. We laughed and clapped as each girl in turn led the class in "Stand up," "Sit down," "Let's go to the market" and all the other phrases they had learned. They were happy that they might someday be teachers, and I was happy with them. Even Abdi the headmaster was happy, for with all the extra work his students were receiving in these summer school classes that I had arranged, he was confident they would do well on the next national exams. I felt at least partially vindicated.

Here was the East African mosaic—Somalia, Kenya, Uganda, Tanzania, Zanzibar. I wanted to shout it to the world, "Look! Just look at all the amazing cultures embraced here. Look at the future!" I knew the future would change in Somalia. Just as I had seen glimpses of the future in other parts of East Africa, I knew that Somalia would take its rightful "future spot" too. What I did not know was just how brutal Somalia's future would become.

I was no starry-eyed first year Peace Corps volunteer. I was much savvier now, and I knew Somalia would have challenges. But not I – not anyone I knew – had a clue as to just how devastating those challenges would be. I simply soaked up this moment, this one moment, knowing it would be brief.

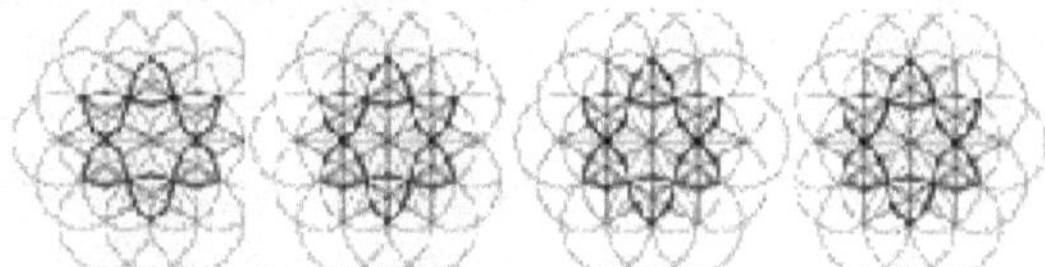

The Never Ending Tale – Part 2

DRAT IT! Hog Face, she with the scrunched-up nose and wicked put downs, was going to corner me again. There was no escaping.

Hog Face was just leaving the home of Conn and Sallie Price, the USAID couple, as I arrived, and we met on the porch.

"Oh, Moriah," Hog Face oozed. "I am so so sorry. Did she die instantly, or later?" There was no sympathy in her voice, only a background sing-song of "Yadda Yadda Yadda – I know a juicy rumor!"

"Neither," I corrected her. "She didn't die at all." Truthfully, I wasn't sure if that was true, for none of us had heard from Susie.

"But she was stabbed, wasn't she?" Hog Face insisted. "In her own bed even! By a Somali man!" Her voice turned very conspiratorial, saying "You remember what I told you about being too friendly with Somali men, don't you, dear?"

Hog Face's cloying voice slithered up and down my spine. I was so angry with her. How did she even hear this rumor? I had only just heard it myself, and the attack had happened about three months earlier. And it was the Peace Corps! Drat it, I should know about it before Hog Face got her claws into the rumor.

"She wasn't too friendly with anyone," I nearly shouted. "It was a stranger who climbed over her fence and broke into her house." I lied – I didn't know that to be true at all.

Sallie, bless her heart, saw how distressed I was when I appeared on her doorstep, promptly ushering me into her house, and nearly slamming the door on Hog Face's nose. "We'll talk another time," Sallie told Hog Face.

Sallie was a softly padded, grandmotherly type, with shoulders as broad as the prairie she was raised on. Conn and Sallie would be leaving in a few weeks. Conn's tour for USAID was coming to an end, and a retirement house was waiting for them in Paradise, California. As Sallie and I sat on her sofa, I buried my face on one of those broad shoulders and cried. Just cried. I didn't know why I was so upset. I barely knew Susie, the Peace Corps volunteer who was stabbed.

She was nice enough, I guess, but we never connected. She was from Indiana and wore the grand smile of a happy country farm girl. She once said that her whole town came out to the Greyhound bus depot to see her off when she left for the Peace Corps, they were so proud of her.

Susie was stationed in a small village south of Mogadishu. Susie and Julia got together from time to time, but even Julia hadn't heard about the incident until the day after it happened, and she heard about it from the Somali teachers at her school – the bush telegraph had shouted the news in record time. The Peace Corps had dispatched a private plane to pick up Susie during the night, and Susie was on her way home to the US before any of us knew she was gone, an all too common Peace Corps tactic. We never even said good bye.

This had all happened in May, before Julia and I went on our wonderful East Africa vacation. I was sad that Julia hadn't told me, so we could cry together, but Julia respected her promise to the Peace Corps to say nothing. The next time I saw Julia, I just hugged her tight and said, "I am so glad you are okay." She hugged me back and softly said, "Thank you."

I was indeed glad that Julia was okay. I was glad that her USAID sweetheart was there to take care of her.

I didn't talk with anyone else about this incident. What needed to be said, had been said. I suspected that Hog Face made it her personal mission to tell everyone in the ex-pat community the story, embellishing it with each telling.

Amazingly, this incident did not stop the Peace Corps from stationing female volunteers in remote posts in Somalia, even in lone posts all by themselves. I discovered later that about one hundred female Peace Corps volunteers throughout the world were sexually assaulted each year, with over twenty of them dying, a stat that did scare the heck out of me. As far as I knew, this was only incident in Somalia.

There were times when I thought that Omar Chicago over-protected Molly and me, building thorn bush fences and chaperoning us whenever someone came to our house, making it difficult for us to learn much about Somali life. But at times like this I truly appreciated his thorn bush fences and his 24-hour guards on our house.

O Holy Night

Freedom and dignity are here,
The two lands are united;
Glory to Allah!
(Anonymous. A Somali song of independence)

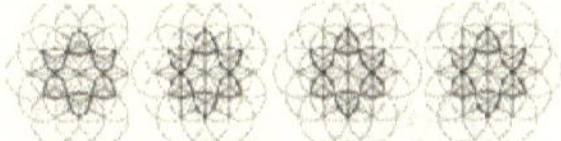

THE AROMA OF ROSES mingled with that of the rich cardamom-laced tea and fresh ginger cookies. Roses nearly always bloomed at the Catholic mission, no matter the season. Today I was having tea with Padre Vittorio, Mario and Sister Teresse, a rare treat.

I knew from the look in the good Padre's eyes that he had an ulterior motive for asking me to stay for tea that day. I had seen that look before, when he first pleaded with me to teach his boys, and I was grateful that he did so, for some of my most joy filled moments came from inside the mission walls. I was accustomed to chatting with Mario in our mutually broken French, but Sister Teresse had never before joined us. I liked all the nuns at the mission, but Sister Teresse was my special favorite. Her sweet innocence belied her seventy or so years, and all her wonderful wrinkles were smiles that she gave everyone. Sister Teresse was the one who first planted the roses in the mission garden, the one who had placed the delicate statue of the Virgin Mary there.

At last Padre Vittorio could hold it in no longer. "*Por favore*," he said, glancing at Mario who translated it all into French for me. "Please. I have a special request. A request for Sister Teresse." The gentle sister smiled and lowered her eyes. "There is a song. A Christmas song. Would you teach it to our boys for Christmas Eve?" He nodded at Mario, and Mario broke into a glorious baritone rendition of

> *"Minuit, chrétiens, c'est l'heure solennelle*
> *Où l'Homme-Dieu descendit jusqu'à nous "*

"Yes!" I smiled, happy. "I know this one. In English it is

> *"O holy night, the stars are brightly shining,*
> *It is the night of our dear savior's birth ..."*

My voice was much quieter and decidedly out of tune, but Sister Teresse beamed as soft tears came to her eyes. I took her hands in mine. "Yes," I said, "we can do this."

Sister Teresse squeezed my hands, then rose and with a quick curtsy mumbled something about "*la cucina*" and left. I didn't ask why this song was important to Sister Teresse; I only knew that this was one small gift I could give, and so, for a few minutes at the end of each class, we practiced singing "O Holy Night." The boys were as enthusiastic as I was about this little project, for they loved Sister Teresse too.

Padre Vittorio didn't have to convince me to stay that afternoon and have another ginger cookie, for there was something I wanted from him as well.

****

Long lay the world in sin and error pining

****

"Padre Vittorio, would you tell me something?"

"Of course," he said. "If I can, I will."

"Can you tell me why Somalis tolerate all of the foreigners in their country? They have a culture that reaches back many centuries – music and religion and government that have served them well for a very long time. Then virtually overnight we have all descended, like a swarm of locusts, to destroy them." This was the one question that had taunted me for months. Why did Somalis tolerate us, even encourage us, to inflict our culture on theirs? "You have been here a long time now. What do you think?"

****

Till He appeared and the soul felt its worth

****

Padre Vittorio paused. I wasn't sure he was even going to try to answer.

"I want to believe," he said, "that our mission is doing good work."

"Oh, yes!" I interjected. "Of course you are. I know you are doing wonderful things here, more than all the rest of us put together. But the others – the Mennonites, the USAID staff, the Russians, the Peace Corps. Why are we here?"

****

The thrill of hope, the weary world rejoiced
As yonder breaks a new and glorious morn

****

Padre Vittorio paused again, choosing his words carefully. "It is the water," he said, "and the oil. Somalia needs water. Somalia wants oil."

A thousand-piece puzzle fell into place. Somalis knew much better than we did that if they but cultivated the respect of a strong foreign nation or two, they could achieve all their dreams. They could have dams and waterways, with all the agriculture that would derive from it, and they could get rich from oil fields, just like other African countries had done.

Reserves rich in oil had already been discovered in countries that Somalia had traded with for millennia. Algeria, Qatar and Oman were filthy rich in oil, and very active drilling was conducted in neighboring Uganda and Kenya. Why not Somalia? Why had Somalia been cheated out of this easy wealth that surrounded them at every turn? Finding oil would solve all the country's problems. Why was this country, once rich in frankincense, myrrh, meerschaum, cattle, and all manner of exotic produce … why was it now so bitterly poor?

That's what the foreigners were doing there. Americans and Russians alike wanted to keep their toes in Somali sand, just in case something rich came to light. So advisors and teachers were sent to Somalia to make contacts. And Somalis tolerated us because they so desperately wanted the oil and water, the riches of the modern world.

It would be nearly fifty years before oil was discovered in Somalia, and a whole lot of grey gunk would run under the bridge before then.

****

Fall on your knees, O hear the angels' voices

****

That was a memorable Christmas. As we entered the church for Christmas Eve services, eight of the agriculture volunteers and me, I saw my boys seated in the front pews, peeking over their shoulders and waving shyly, each wearing new blue shorts with a sparkling white shirt and blue choir style bow, and when they rose to sing the chapel filled with angels. I recall how Sister Teresse gently set a beautifully wrapped rum drenched fruit cake into my hands as we left the church that Christmas Eve.

I remember a thorn bush Christmas tree that the agriculture volunteers brought back from the bush – they set it in our living room and decorated it with old fashioned paper chains that they made.

I remember the toy trucks and yoyos that Molly and I gave the agriculture volunteers who congregated at our house, and the Christmas carols that rang from our home through the wee hours of the morning. On Christmas Day the agriculture volunteers, Molly and I savored the canned ham that the embassy wives in Mogadishu had sent out to us, along with canned beans and fresh potatoes.

But most of all I am haunted by the sadness in Padre Vittorio's eyes as he spoke to me that day by the rose bushes. He knew that "wanting" or even "needing" was not "getting." The social workers who poured into Somalia did not sate Somalia's thirst for either water or wealth.

I knew Padre Vittorio was right, but I had to push it aside. I didn't like being a pawn in the grand game of multi-national oil corporations, and in truth that is all I was, a pawn cultivating the crumbs of friendship. I focused on making life a little bit better for my students, for that was all I knew how to do.

****

O night divine
O night, O holy night

****

Hip Hip Hooray for Bollywood!

"This world is but a fleeting moment, and now our lives are full,
That this prosperity may endure, let us sing 'amen' "(Chorus in traditional Somali song)

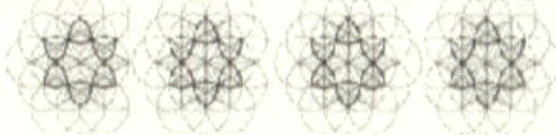

"GOOD HEAVENS, it's 'Born Free' tonight!" I was so excited I was beside myself.

Our days had quickly fallen into a routine – morning classes, afternoon classes and five nights a week we taught adult evening classes. But tonight was our free night, and here was a special treat just waiting for us!

Molly and I stood outside the amphitheater where movies were shown most nights. We had just left a tea cafe in the village, quenching our thirst with an afternoon spot of tea, the sweet cardamom tea that I had come to relish. Molly hadn't wanted to go for tea, but I wasn't wild about sitting there by myself, so I met her after her afternoon class and talked her into it.

We sat outdoors at a table by ourselves, as we always did. We were the only women at the tea cafe, as we always were, except for the waitress. Kadija, the waitress, was an older woman, probably in her thirties although she looked much older. Her near toothless grin greeted us as we entered, and she immediately shooed a group of men away from the table under the massive oak tree so we could sit in the shade. Kadija's dress always looked filthy, stained with bits of food and goodness knows what else, but her grin was genuine, inspired no doubt by the generous tip I always left. Kadija might have come from a poor family, working to support them. Or her boisterous spirit suggested she might have run away from her village, perhaps to avoid injustices, perhaps to find a better life. No matter her reason for being at the tea cafe, I liked her.

Tea cafes nestled in every possible corner of every town all over Somalia. There were probably a dozen or so in Baidoa, but this is the one I liked, probably because Kadija always took good care of us. Tea cafes throughout Somalia served sizzling cardamom tea in thick squat glasses, and for lunch and dinner served a thinly sliced "beefsteak" cooked to charcoal perfection, served with rice or spaghetti. On Tifu's day off we often set off for this tea café for dinner.

This particular afternoon was quite lovely, and Molly chatted away about her classes back in the States where she was an honored teacher. As usual, her skirt was much too short and too tight, but that was Molly. She still wore lipstick and put a bit of blush to accent the dimple on her chin, but that was just Molly too.

"When Mr. Whitsom announced that I was named the Top Teacher for the second year in a row, I was simply speechless." Molly's creativity and dedication had apparently bowled over her administrative staff.

I was more intrigued with the Somalis passing by. I noticed the young men, and older ones too, who walked by, casually holding hands. There was no homosexuality in Somalia, but holding hands seemed to be okay. I didn't see women holding hands, just men. It struck me as odd, but it was one of those customs I simply accepted.

"Don't you agree?" Molly was waving a piece of paper, something she had gotten in a letter we picked up from the post office.

"Sure," I said. "That's nice." Truthfully, I hadn't a clue what she was talking about. I had been watching a young crippled boy maneuver his way through groups of men, expertly placing his primitive crutches for support, pausing to pick up pennies they gave him. This is the same boy who met us most afternoons as school let out, and I always gave him something. One of the teachers got very angry with me, saying I gave him too much. "How much is too much," I wondered, "for people who have so little?"

"It's not nice at all!" Molly hit the table with her fist. "You're not even listening to me."

She was right; I wasn't listening to her. Now that she had my attention, she continued, "This linen company, the one I paid hundreds of dollars to, just so they would embroider my linen with my new initial when I got married … this linen company wants to go ahead and initial my linens with "L", from my maiden name. I've never heard of such a thing. It is not nice at all."

Molly was thirty years old, with no marriage in sight, so I didn't see the problem. But I didn't say anything. I did wonder if perhaps she joined the Peace Corps to find the husband she hadn't found in college.

Our path home took us past the amphitheater. We had been to the movies several times, and we were always the only women there, the men giving us lots of elbow room to ensure they didn't touch us. The open air theater held about two hundred people on wooden benches lined up in haphazard rows up a gentle hillside. Usually the two rows below us, and the two rows above us were all empty, giving us lots of room to stretch. There were typically only two kinds of movies shown: Bollywood musicals and "spaghetti westerns."

I liked the Bollywood musicals the best. They were in Arabic, sometimes with Italian subtitles, with lots of singing and dancing and pretty women in rather skimpy outfits. I couldn't tell one plot from another, they were all just singing and dancing, but the costumes were pretty.

The spaghetti westerns were cowboy tales shot in Italy. Personally I thought they should leave the bangbangshootumups to the real West. They all had pretty much the same plot too, and were filmed in Italian, sometimes with Arabic subtitles.

"Born Free" was a delightful surprise.

We took Greg with us to the movie that evening. Greg was one of the agriculture volunteers and after a day of shopping for supplies in Baidoa, he was spending the night, bunking at our house. The agriculture volunteers knew our door was always open to them, and the spare room was theirs. Dusk came at six o'clock in Baidoa, no matter the season, so the movie always started at seven. As we entered the gate, we saw that the theater was jammed to the gills with about two hundred Somali men except for a few spots right smack dab in the middle. We had never seen it so packed.

"Look!" said Abdulazziz, the proprietor. "All Somalis know this is good movie. You say it is good movie!" He waved his arms over the crowd.

I smiled at the thought that so many men came to the movie because word got out that the American women liked this film, not realizing that it was simply a story about a lion.

Men jostled about, giving us plenty of room to reach our seats, the seats on the long backless bench right in the middle that they had saved for us, and as we sat down, the movie began.

The titles came up … in Italian. The credits came up … in Italian. Actors began to speak, and we discovered it was entirely dubbed, in Italian, with no subtitles at all.

No matter, we loved it, and we clapped wildly at the end, as did everyone else.

Warriors, Wanderers and Very Wicked Women

Birds perched together on the same tree
Call each their own cries,
Each country has its own ways
Indeed people do not understand each other's talk.
("Fortitude", a Somali folk song)

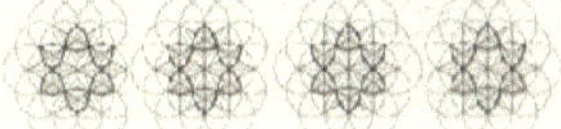

THEY STOOD THERE. Eight of them in a semi-circle facing Molly and me. Eight young Rahanweyn warriors with huge immaculate hair poufs and redgreenblue wraparounds in patterns of plaids and stripes. Each held a long walking stick in one hand; the other hand was tucked inside a shawl loosely draped over one shoulder, with glints of silver shooting out, reflections from knife blades in the midday sun. These were the young protectors of the region, the warriors flaunting their masculinity and their eligibility.

They took a step toward us in synchronized motion. A few more silver streaks shot out.

We froze. We had just emerged from a tiny shop in Gorsony village. We heard the door close behind us and everyone backed away.

The day had begun so sedately … an adventure to a remote village. Before sunrise we had piled into Scott's Land Rover, the one the Peace Corps had assigned Scott for his agriculture work along the edges of Baidoa. It was Friday, our day off, and we were actually going to visit a small village, a first for Molly and me.

Baidoa was small, but it was a town with about thirty small shops and half a dozen outdoor cafes, even a hotel. Baidoa's hotel was a row of six small rooms, each with a single bed and a window. All the guests, if there were any, shared the long drop in the yard. A "long drop" was the African version of the Indian squat poddy, essentially an eight- to twelve-foot deep hole in the ground. The hotel's long drop was an especially luxurious one – it was surrounded by adobe walls for privacy and even had a roof. The roof kept out the rain, but kept in the odors. The very tight quarters led to a massive stench, but it was indeed state of the art architecture in the bush country.

Baidoa was proud too of its many tailors who could copy any garment in a fabric of your choice, turning vibrant geometric prints and stunning florals into dresses and shirts in just a few minutes.

Baidoa also bragged about its sandal makers who crafted leather sandals just for your foot.

Baidoa was most proud of the mosque with a minaret that towered over the town, calling men to worship five times a day. An *iman*, a holy man, stood on the top balcony and with a loud megaphone announced the times for prayer. All the men of the village had to get there in time for the ritual washing before they took their places on the woven mats. One day I was walking out of the market area about noon and one of my students introduced me to his cousins who were visiting, true young Rahanweyn warriors, the ones with the immaculate huge hair styles, the first I had actually met. I held out my hand to shake theirs, as was quite customary, and with a noticeable hesitation they each shook mine. Sadly I discovered that shaking my hand meant that they would have to go back and re-do the ritual washing before going to the mosque, for touching a woman renders a man unworthy of participating in prayer.

When Scott, a Peace Corps Volunteer in the agriculture contingent, asked Molly and me if we would like to visit a real bush village, we absolutely jumped at the chance. We had never seen a true bush village, and we certainly had never devoted a few hours exploring one, so this was a splendid break from our routine.

We headed off about 5:00 am, an hour before the sun crept out for another day. Sayyed, our driver, worked at the USAID demonstration farm on the outskirts of Baidoa and spoke very good English. Ronny, another visiting Peace Corps agriculture volunteer from a lone post, was spending a few days in Baidoa, and he went along too. I sometimes wondered how the volunteers in lone posts saved their sanity. There was no one for them to talk to, with few diversions in the small villages they were posted to. While visiting a small village was an adventure for me, it was a way of life for them. We all piled in for the three-hour trip, the men in front, Molly and me in back. We had extra water and gas, but little else. Like the camel-herding nomads sprinkled through the bush country, we trusted in Allah to get us there and back again.

The first few miles of the dirt road were relatively smooth, but then we abruptly turned into a camel path of potholes. This was the Cement Mixer ride at the Santa Cruz Boardwalk back home, a jostling and jolting that seemed would never stop. The guys, full of bravado, laughed their way through it. Molly was pea green, and I suspect I sported some vile shade of khaki.

The sun broke the morning haze, shooting thousands of spears of gold into the sky as we ventured further into the bush. We did spot bits of wildlife, making the whole trip worthwhile as far as I was concerned. The tiny two-foot tall dhig dhig, elfin deer-like creatures, jumped through bushes as if on tiny trampolines.

Ronny claimed to see the golden eyes of big cat, a lion perhaps. There was no *libaah* today. *"Libaah"* means both "lion" and "shark" in Somali. Once a Somali peddler came to our house in Baidoa with an assortment of carvings he had done. I had never before met, nor would I ever again meet, an artisan like this man. There were no "art galleries" or "craft shops" in the entire country. The art that existed was functional, like the carvings on wood pillows or the weaving on prayer mats. Here was an artist, an itinerate sales person, who created art for pure decoration. I bought a small *"libaah"* from him. Its sleek lines suggested a shark, but the crisscross design around its neck was a mane for certain. I don't know if this artisan knew how perfectly he captured both creatures. My *libaah* still sits in my cabinet of special treasures. Perhaps if we had travelled at night we could have seen this dark predator.

"Watch out!" Ronny jumped when he pointed to a cobra, poised to lunge at our Land Rover. Ronny was seated on the right-hand side, on the outside of the open sided vehicle. I sat just behind him, and I was also very vulnerable if the cobra struck. Blessedly, that danger too passed.

An amazing variety of wildlife inhabited the thorn bushes and trees. Our Land Rover made so much noise clamoring along that we scared away most of them, but we did catch glimpses of gazelle leaping over thorn bushes, and statuesque kudu with their distinctive brown and white striping. The grand curvy horn of the kudu was used as a shofar by the Yemenite Jews of northern Somalia to waken the New Year on Rosh Hashanah. Some scholars suggested that the Yemenite Jews were in fact the Lost Tribe of Israel.

The reedbuck may have been there amongst the thorn bushes too, but its reddish coat blended so well with the adobe-colored soil that we wouldn't have seen it.

Just before reaching the village, we mercifully made a poddy stop. The guys headed off to the left, while Molly and I went to the right. With the car motor turned off, we heard the morning song of the Somali lark, no doubt alerting the forest to the arrival of this strange creature that spilled its children off on each side.

The dense six-foot tall thorn bushes scratched and pricked us through our cotton skirts and blouses, and with all our turning and twisting, in no short order we were lost. In spite of the songs of the larks, this was an un-fun stop. Neither Molly nor I had the foresight to even bring a roll of toilet paper. First I kept watch for her, then she kept watch for me. I am not certain just what we were watching for, since there was little we could do against any wild game. I was certain that she would not do battle against any creature on my behalf, and, I suspect, I would do no more for her. I think we were watching to make sure that no other cobras lurked about. If we had seen a cobra, or anything else, perhaps one of us would have made it out alive.

We started back, or so we thought, but it was only with the guys honking the horn of the Land Rover that we got our bearings again.

Sayyed was clearly shaken. He hustled us into the Land Rover and truly sped away. The guys had run across fresh tracks of *libaah*, and none of them had so much as a bow and arrow.

Gorsony shot into view unexpectedly, round adobe huts with pointed thatched roofs, in a few acres meticulously cleared of scrub brush and thorns, perhaps 70 or 80 huts altogether. Gorsony, had none of Baidoa's amenities – few shops, no tailors, no sandal makers, no hotel, and certainly no mosque. Most of the huts were grouped into compounds of three to six huts. Sayyed seemed to know where he was going as he expertly navigated around curious children and goats, delivering us to the edge of the chief's compound.

An older man came out with a broad, nearly toothless, smile and open arms. His clay-colored wraparound was secured at his waist with a rope.

Everyone cleared a path for him, and for us, so we knew immediately that he was the chief of the village.

"Chief" is a loose term in a village like this; it is a term of respect granted to an older man who has earned that recognition through his wisdom. The chief in rural Somalia is the arbiter of village disputes and typically represents the villagers in inter-tribal disputes, like the theft of another tribe's cows or camels. The village unit is the strong familial and legal entity that holds individuals accountable. Not only do villagers share the wealth and hardship of their collective experience, but they also hold each other accountable for the welfare of the tribe. A wrong doer was always expected to make amends, whether the wrong was committed against someone in the village or someone in another village. When a penalty was especially strong, such as for the theft of crops in a drought-driven season, the whole village would combine its resources to make amends to the wronged, typically granting camels or goats or harvested grains to one who was wronged. The village stood behind the wrong doer in all but two instances: When the wrong doer became too severe a financial burden on the village, and when the wrong doer exhibited fraudulent and deceitful intent. The honor of Somalis was so strong that they simply would not tolerate fraud and deceit in their midst, and the deceitful person was banished forever.

All of that changed of course under European domination when "justice" meant that the wrong doer was sent to prison, and no reparation was ever allotted to the wronged. The old tribal system still survived in Somalia in bush country villages like Gorsony and, I suspect, also amongst the camel herding nomads.

A babble broke out in the chief's compound with Sayyed shouting about the *libaah*, and others responding with arms waving. Sayyed calmed down and told us that the Chief was aware of the danger and expected a group of hunters to arrive the next day. The lion had in fact already killed two cows in the region and was considered a major threat.

We were all invited into the chief's compound where sweet cardamom laced black tea and scone-like bread waited for us. These were fine gifts indeed from bush people, for cardamom and sugar would have been in short supply so far from a trading village like Baidoa. We all sat cross legged on a woven rug, likely made from the stalks and leaves of maize; its purple and aqua diamond design sprinting across the rectangle, a pattern reminiscent of that found in Navajo rugs.

Molly and I sat with the men while the women of the compound scurried to serve us. This was a very typical reaction to Peace Corps women, in fact to all European women. We ate with the men whether we were at a restaurant or at someone's home, with a full meal or a cup of tea. The Somali women served us, then later they ate whatever was left over. I caused a mini uproar once when I tried to eat with the women. The head of the household felt insulted, as if his hospitality wasn't good enough, and the women simply did not know what to do with me. It was very awkward all the way around.

Although few Somalis had any idea what the Peace Corps was doing, especially the Peace Corps women, everyone assumed that we were very wealthy, no matter our background, so we were granted the privileges of the ruling class.

The men soon headed off to talk about agriculture, which was after all the purpose of our visit. The assumption was that Molly and I would remain in the compound, and perhaps even take a nap. We had other ideas.

We had glimpsed a watering hole as we came into the village and I wanted to sketch the women there, so we headed off, with Aisha, the chief's wife, close behind, dressed in a wrapped dress with a faded blue design. It was probably the best dress she owned. We invited Aisha to walk beside us, but she declined. She knew that we were Miriam Yahr and Miriam Weyn, but our conversation was very limited. I silently cursed my very basic language skills, for I wanted so much to talk with this woman, to discover what her dreams were for her children, to ask about any family treasures that might be in her care, and so much more. I wanted to know what was important to her. I knew she was a very kind woman, a strong woman, and I wanted her to think well of me too.

I was hoping that my sketchbook might ease some of the communication issues. Aisha and I sat on a little hill a bit away from the water hole, tucking our long skirts around our legs, and I took out my sketch book and pencil and began my simple drawing. Molly wandered around, searching for somewhere to settle where her too short skirt wouldn't slide up her naked thigh. She finally sat on a patch of grass, naked legs and all. On an adjacent small hill several boys were engaged in wooden sword play, forming teams and chasing each other, using a rivulet from the water hole as the territorial dividing line. Nearby a group of girls, perhaps six to ten years old, played with dolls, stones wrapped in bits of cloth. They seemed to be building a pretend fire and cooking something for their children, spirited discussions determining what to cook. These little brothers and sisters were solving the problems of their universe, just as my siblings and I had solved ours in very different surroundings. The topics on both playgrounds weren't that different at all.

The water hole area itself seemed to have three distinct sections, one for camels, cattle and goats to be watered; one for women to draw water for drinking and cooking; and one area by the side where women beat fabrics against stones worn smooth over the centuries. There were about a dozen women there that morning. They all wore nearly identical wrapped dresses, all well-worn and dyed shades of brown from the earth they walked on, with hints of pink and blue and yellow flowers that once were there. Their water buckets were made from kerosene cans or goat skins.

I did know enough to not draw the faces of any of the women, for the Koran forbade any image of a person. So my sketches were of the sloping rocks, of the curved backs of the women gathering water, of the round thorn bushes bordering the area. The rhythm of the women washing clothes, their shoulders swaying gently in a timeless arc, formed a counterpoint to the lowering and raising of the water buckets. The women did not sing out loud, but sometimes hummed softly, and they rarely even spoke, but the music was understood. The music had been there for so many millennia that no one had to hear it aloud to know it was there.

There was a Spirit at the springs too, a Spirit that had been there for all time. Perhaps it was Goddess Arawello herself. Perhaps it was another Spirit. Whoever it was, she arched her arms over the water hole, embracing all, echoing an aura of peace.

I wanted so badly to be part of this coterie of women that I did something that surprised even me. I stood and walked slowly to the water's edge. Aisha raised her eyebrows in alarm, but followed me. At the pond, I knelt and held out my hand to one of the women, asking for a piece of cloth to wash. She handed me a dim yellow scarf. All the women fell silent. I dipped the scarf into the pool, and very softly, in rhythm with my washing, I sang,

"This is the way we wash our clothes,
Wash our clothes, wash our clothes,
This is the way we wash our clothes
All on a Monday morning."

That old nursery rhyme sprang out of my deep memory. I smiled, and glancing around the circle I saw the other women smiling. Then they began to wash their clothes in rhythm with my little song. The women's thread that held us together reached around the pond, tugging at all of our hearts. That was the moment that I felt closest to Somali women. Never before, nor after, did I know that women's connection, the connection that transcended time and culture.

After a few minutes, I stopped, and smiling, I motioned for them to sing. Aisha knelt beside me, and taking a piece of washing herself, she began a joyful song, a call-and-response song that everyone knew. I joined them as I kept time with my washing, everyone smiling, everyone laughing.

Here was the true poetry of Somalia. The poetry was simply there. Always. Some of the long epic poems have been translated into English, but here was the true poetry of these people, the chants and melodies that framed each moment of their lives. Men might wax lyrical about the beauty of a camel or the bravery of an army captain, but here the songs were written by the soul. In all the time I was in Somalis, this was when I regretted the most that I could not understand the Somali language. I wanted so desperately to know what they singing … yet from deep inside I knew they sang of the beauty of the world, of the goodness of Allah, perhaps even of Arawello. I felt at peace.

One little lad pointed up. "Look!" he said, as he pointed to a cloud. *"Libaah!"*

"No, no," said his older sister as she covered his hand and brought it down. "Don't point at the sky, for the clouds might be frightened and bring us no rain."

As the sun rose in the sky, I returned to our bit of grass to retrieve my drawing paper and pencil, and one young girl of about eight edged boldly up beside me. I don't know if she had seen a picture of any kind before, and she didn't seem at all to recognize the scene I was sketching. I smiled at her, and she quietly smiled back, her huge eyes peeking at this thing on my lap. I held out my pencil for her, but she put her hands behind her slender back. I took out a clean piece of paper and showed her how to draw a line. She furrowed her brow as she looked at the line, and didn't seem to know what I was doing.

"Nabud mia?" I said. *Is there peace?* She looked puzzled and shuffled her toes in the loose soil.

"Maga ai guwa Miriam Yahr. Ad na?" My name is *Little Miriam. What's yours?*

I didn't discover until decades later that my little friend probably didn't understand me, for I was speaking a language she did not know. I was speaking the language of Hargeisa, of northern Somalia, and the people of Gorsony spoke the language of the Upper Juba region in southern Somalia. But this child didn't have a chance to reply for her mother had scurried up and gently shuffled her away, water spilling from her pails in her rush. She was a brave little girl and I couldn't help but wonder what her life would have been like if she had been born in a town like Baidoa, let alone in a western town. She was not unhappy, her eyes were bright. She was alert and curious. She didn't know any other way of life, had no knowledge of the world outside of Gorsony. She hadn't even seen the spaghetti westerns and Bollywood musical movies that we saw in Baidoa. She would marry young, probably bringing her own children to this same water hole, and like all Somalis everywhere in the country she would sometimes find the spring dry or filled with vermin-laden mud. I was angry with the Peace Corps and all the other interlopers. Here we were, educating the country's elite, when what these kind and generous people truly needed was a reliable source of water.

"Stop it!" Molly suddenly screamed, as a few pebbles landed near her, someone deliberately tossing them in her direction. Aisha rushed over to stop the commotion.

"You nasty kids!" shouted Molly. "Don't you have any manners?" I was so glad that Aisha did not understand English, for the children weren't nasty at all. The pebbles might even have come from some of the women nearby who objected to Molly's bare legs and the fact that her underwear was visible when she pulled her knees to her chest.

Thankfully it was late morning and Molly, the indefatigable shopper, reminded me that we wanted to visit the little village before noon. We suspected that the shops closed for midday prayers and lunch, the main meal of the day, and wouldn't re-open until the next day. A brisk ten minute walk took us to the center of the shopping area.

Popular Somali music blared from transistor radios at the open market on the far side where the merchants, many of them women, were packing up their wares. The transistor radio phenomenon never ceased to astound me. Here we were, in the middle of thorn bush country, and the transistors blared with music and news, just like they did in Baidoa. Everyone it seemed – merchants, camel herders, people walking the village roads – everyone had a radio blaring. No, not everyone had a transistor radio. Every man seemed to have a transistor radio; the women did not.

A group of four small shops stood nearby, just a few feet from the open market. One of the Gorsony shop keepers seemed especially anxious for us to see his wares, so we smiled at his invitation and went in.

The shop was so tiny that only Molly and I could fit inside. Aisha waited outside for us. Inside that tiny shop in the middle of bush country was one of the biggest surprises of my entire tour in Somalia. Draped across the tins of tomato paste and ghee was a huge woman's bra, probably at least a size 44DDD, and it was a bright red. The shopkeeper grinned from ear to ear as he showed it to us. Molly feigned embarrassment, and I simply burst out laughing. How any shopkeeper anywhere in Somalia could have come across this item was beyond my imagination.

Ali the shopkeeper had some tea ready for us, and we graciously accepted his hospitality. As we sipped our tea, he showed us tin after tin of merchandise and we ended up buying several tins of goodness knows what. The tins were from Egypt with small pictures of beans and vegetables we couldn't begin to identify. We did not buy that bra. With tears of laughter slipping down my face, we bade our host *"Amana Allah"*, *Go with God*, and stepped outside.

Swinging around to the side of the shop we froze.

There, straight in front of us, about ten yards away, was the semi-circle of Rahanweyn warriors. I had seen dozens of these warriors in Baidoa and I had never before felt afraid. I was accustomed to seeing young Rahanweyn warriors carrying their wooden pillow in one hand, and a spear in the other. I was not accustomed to the seething anger in their eyes, and I tensed with fear. The warriors held spears with tips dipped in poison. The spears pointed to the sky, and a taut alertness ensured that they could have thrown those spears at our hearts in an instant.

In synchronized motion they took a step toward us. I looked around for Aisha, but she was nowhere to be seen. We couldn't retreat into the shop, for the door had closed behind us.

Molly started waving her arms. "No! No! Don't hurt me!" Molly cried out. "Here, take my money!" and she held out her handbag, waving it frantically for them to take.

I grabbed her flailing arms. "Stop. They don't understand. Stop! Listen to me." I shook her to get her attention, and I said as calmly as I could muster, "Take one step backward. Here we go ... step." I stood shoulder to shoulder with Molly and we both took one step backward. And the warriors all took one step toward us.

"Again, Molly. Just one slow step backward. Here we go ... step." We took a second step backward. And again the warriors took a step toward us, slowing closing in.

"*Nabud mia?*" I ventured. *Is there peace?*

I got no response. I assumed that they understood me, but in retrospect there is a good possibility that they didn't understand me at all.

I tried again. "*Nabud mia?*"

Not an expression changed. Not a finger moved.

"*Ma fiee da?*" I tried saying another version of the greeting. The warriors should have responded "*Wan fia,*" but they said nothing. They just kept staring at us. I absolutely did not know what to do. Running was not an option, nor could we remain as we were. This was not a time for smiling, but I held out my hands to show that we had no weapons, we meant no harm. I nudged Molly to do the same. I couldn't fathom why this was happening. We were guests of the village chief. Nor did it seem reasonable that the growing political unrest had reached this far into the bush to focus on us.

Did the warriors know we were infidels? Did they know we were uncircumcised teachers … teachers corrupting their women? What had we done that made them feel so violent toward us?

We heard a commotion behind us and I knew we were surrounded. The headline flashed across my mind: *Two Peace Corps Women Killed by Somali Warriors.* I felt a rush of hot air crackle beside me as one of those from behind rushed forward. Energy poured out of me like a busted dam and I nearly fainted. Thankfully, the rush of electric air was the village chief marching toward the warriors. He took a stance in between the young warriors and us, his arms held out like a human shield. He spoke, then put his arms down at his side. After some more conversation, the young Rahanweyn warriors turned and with long strides walked away, without so much as a backward glance. My knees got weak. Relief and fear and immense gratitude all hit me simultaneously.

The chief motioned for us to follow him. We went back to his compound where Scott, Ronny and Sayyed were waiting.

"What a stupid thing to do."

"You could have gotten us all killed!"

"Haven't you got a brain in your head?"

Scott and Ronny threw a slew of ill will at us and I finally shouted, "Stop it! Stop. We went into the village to visit a shop. We visited a shop. Aisha was with us. What was so wrong with that?"

Sayyed stepped forward as the voice of reason. "The people in the village know you are guests of the chief. These men are not of this village. They are the hunters. They kill the lion. They don't know you."

Sayyed paused, looking confused. He took Scott aside and spoke to him softly. Scott came back with a smirk on his face. "In their village," Scott related," a woman was once an adulteress, and the husband threw boiling water on her, blotching her skin white. You are all white."

Scott stopped, quietly laughing under his breath. He leaned into us, whispering, "So, no, you didn't know what the devil you were doing, you wicked wicked women." Scott clearly enjoyed his moment of superiority. Holy cow! I wanted to slug him.

I felt humiliated that Scott was the one to tell us that, but I knew that Sayyed would never take the liberty of saying something like that to a white woman -- he held us in too much regard.

The chief offered us tea and something to eat. A goat had been killed and had been cooking all morning, a feast in our honor. I watched as the others gathered around the large platter of rice and goat, sitting on the woven rug. I just sipped tea. No doubt the goat was very good, but I just couldn't eat. The full impact of our little adventure hit my gut. My stomach was in knots. I felt terrible that I might offend the chief and I asked Sayyed to convey my regrets. The chief nodded at me like he would nod at a wayward child. The chief didn't seem too concerned; after all, I was a foreign woman, and I behaved strangely.

Two other guests joined everyone at the feast, an itinerate sandal maker who travelled from village to village making and repairing sandals, and a *wadaad*, a member of one of the religious groups that belonged to no tribe who performed marriage rites, burial ceremonies and birth blessings for all villages. Being enemies of none, these travelers were welcomed by all. Each carried the tools of his trade -- the sandal maker had leather goods; the *wadaad* carried his Koran in a cloth bag, a prayer rug made of fine leather, a Moslem rosary and some paper for writing. If a *wadaad* were a healer, he would carry his medicinal herbs as well, and some practiced divination through written works in Arabic or reading geometric designs.

Neither the sandal maker nor the *wadaad* carried provisions of any kind, relying instead on the hospitality of villagers. They were indeed treated as honored members of the extended family, as is the tradition throughout Somalia. Hospitality, a strong tenet of Somali life, meant that every door was open to a traveler, every meal was to be shared, no matter how meager. The sandal maker and the *wadaad* were infrequent, but very honored guests.

As the meal ended, Sayyed looked up at the sky and said that we had to leave immediately, that rain was coming in. We tendered our many thanks to the Chief for his hospitality, and for his intervention with the warriors. I asked if I could go find Aisha and thank her, for she was the one who had run to get help when Molly and I were in danger, but Sayyed said No, that we had to leave at once.

So we piled into the Land Rover again, and none too soon. Within half an hour the rain poured down. This whole region was bush country, a desert, and the powerful rains always caught me off guard. In Baidoa it tended to downpour for two to four hours most afternoons during the rainy seasons, then stop abruptly. This day was a long rain, and it poured and poured. First the windshield wipers stopped working. Then we all got soaked from the open sided vehicle.

Then the Land Rover got stuck in a clay sort of mud, really stuck. We all piled out. We took positions around the Land Rover and pushed it out of the mud-soaked rut, then piled back in. Not five minutes later it got stuck again. And again. And again. Each time we all piled out, we all pushed, and we all got back in.

Molly had worn her sweet little strappy sandals with the pink flowers and was spending more time digging the sandals out of the mud than she was helping with the Land Rover. At one point she saw my sturdy sandals, shoes that I had bought at a men's shoe store in New York.

"Those are lesbian shoes." Molly sneered and wrinkled her nose. I bristled at her assessment, and she giggled, amused beyond reason.

"No, they are men's sandals," said Ronny. "I've got a pair just like them."

Good grief, were we going to take a vote on it? Was Molly just taunting me, or did she really figure it out?

"They are comfortable shoes," I said as calmly as I could muster. Drat it, Molly had been a rotten ass that whole day, baring her legs (and underwear) in public, freaking out when we met the young Rahanweyn warriors, giggling at the goat feast, and now this shoe thing. Drat it, I really wanted to shove her dimples into the mud, but too many people were watching.

Soon the Land Rover hit a pothole that we just couldn't get it out of, no matter what we did. We were all sickenly muddy, punched with thorn bush holes, sweaty, and exhausted.

Oh nooo, they were there again. We were surrounded by young Rahanweyn warriors. Again. Afro hairdos popped up all over, six of them. But these were not the same young warriors that we had encountered that morning. It was a different group, with worn faded loin cloths and Afro hair styles, now disheveled.

Sayyed called out to them and explained our predicament. This time the warriors put their shoulders to the Land Rover and, along with the strength of Scott, Ronny and Sayyed, they pushed the Land Rover out of the pothole. We didn't test fate by jumping back into the Land Rover, so we stayed out and slogged our way through. Only Sayyed got into the Land Rover as the driver.

I expected the warriors to wave good bye and head off on their way, but they didn't. For the next five hours these young warriors walked with us, and every few minutes they put their shoulders to the Land Rover and dug it out of yet another pothole, all along chanting a song that Sayyed knew too. I don't know whether to call it incredible graciousness, stubbornness, bravado, or sheer guts, but these warriors were not going to let us get stuck in thorn bush country.

Finally we came to the main road and, although it too was a dirt road, it was more stable. We thanked these good men profusely. They declined our offer of money. *"Amana Allah,"* they called out as they waved and headed back into the bush.

"Amana Allah," we called after them. *Go with God.*

So in the span of a few hours young Rahanweyn warriors had nearly killed Molly and me, and other set of Rahanweyn warriors had rescued us from a very precarious situation;

… I refrained from slugging an obnoxious Peace Corps volunteer;

… I joined Somali women in song;

… we had seen a huge red bra in a tiny shop in bush country;

… and one little girl saw the smiles of a friendly white woman.

As I fell into bed very late that night, I put this day on the plus side of the ledger.

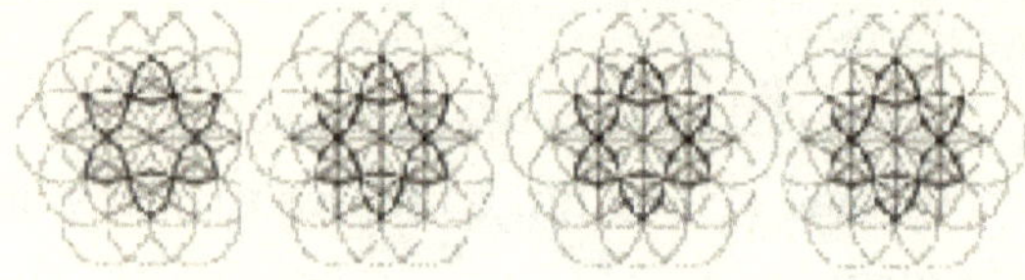

The Gift of Wisdom, Re-telling a Somali Fable

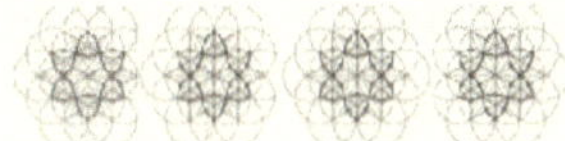

IN THE BEGINNING of time, the Great Spirit
wanted to grant Wisdom to His creations, so He
created a beautiful blue lake where he put all the
wisdom of the world. He told all of His creatures to
go and drink from this Lake of Wisdom.

First the animals went toward the lake. The
Great Spirit had created a special pool for animals
where they could go and drink of special knowledge,
knowledge of the other creatures, the forests, the
deserts. The animals drank deeply and became very
wise in their ways.

Next the men went to the lake and drank
vigorously. After having their fill, they sat by the lake,
chatted and chewed *q'at*, the narcotic leaf chewed in

dens, much like the opium dens of the Arabic world. That is how men came to have wisdom, but the *q'at* muddled their minds and so their wisdom was never put to good use.

Finally the women were allowed to go to the lake. They had little time to drink the waters of wisdom for their children called and many womanly duties pulled them from this pleasure. They had only taken but a few sips when they dashed off to teach their children all the wisdom they had. The women's wisdom became the most valuable wisdom of all, for all the women's wisdom is shared, passed from generation to generation.

(When I first heard this story, the animals were granted no knowledge at all, and women gained only enough knowledge to be considered flighty and uninformed. Men were given all the knowledge they could ever desire, and so they were designated the leaders of society. But that was a tale told by men many years ago.

Perhaps it is time to hear the women's version of the story. ~Miriam Yahr)

The Preying Mantis

Women are the devil's snares.
~ Somali proverb

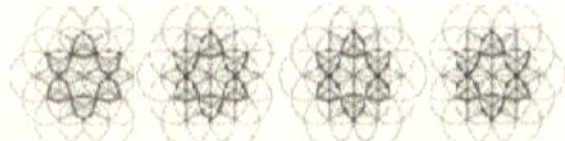

GREY SHADOWS stretched across the long white adobe wall, breaking into distorted figures as they wandered over tables and chairs. So this was the Lido.

The Lido hugged the shore of the Indian Ocean on the outskirts of Mogadishu, alone, like no other business wanted to associate with it. It was the pick-up joint where Somali girls went to find their sugar daddies, where they went to escape their impoverished lives, or simply to survive. My male friends wouldn't tell me where the Lido was, but my taxi driver knew exactly where to go. As he pulled up in front of the flashing red and yellow neon sign, he turned around and said, "Is this where you want to go?" I assured him that it was indeed where I wanted to go.

"I Can't Get No Satisfaction" blared at me as I entered. "So true," I thought. I wasn't happy with my life in Somalia, I bungled everything I tried. My only true success came when I made peanut butter from scratch – everyone loved it. Other than that, my teaching was mediocre, my social life was non-existent, my accomplishments were pretty close to zilch. I felt strangely drawn to these women, women whose lives were dangling by a noxious thread -- not a sexual draw, but an emotional one. I blithely assumed I might connect with one or two of these women, and actually help them.

As I walked into this notoriously seedy joint, raging testosterone hit me, flinging from the walls and dripping from the dingy Chinese lanterns that lit the shadowy space, rather like a side show game of paint balls run amok.

The men at the bar puffed out their chests like orangutans trying to impress a female of the species. The men were of all ages, all sizes and shapes, all nationalities, Europeans, Arabs, Americans and Somalis. Most were dressed casually with cotton slacks and short sleeved shirts. A few wore suits, some in all white suits. Sadly, I recognized a number of my Peace Corps male colleagues. All the men were there for one reason: to have sex with one of the Somali women. It was a week night, a Wednesday, and the Lido was stuffed with two hundred or more people.

I secured a spot at the far end of the bar, ordered a glass of mediocre wine, hoping I wouldn't be too conspicuous. I need not have worried – no one cast me so much as a glance.

As the band began playing "Ticket to Ride," I surveyed the women. The Somali girls were, for the most part, very pretty, and some were quite beautiful, with huge dark eyes set in a mocha-toned face with soft features. Most were slender. In fact, most Somali women in general were slender, partly due to inherited genes, and partly due to their meager diet. Some of the Lido women wore the vibrant colors of the Somali wraparound dress, perhaps with gold jewelry on their ear lobes, or on their arms. Some were dressed in more western attire, with low cut necklines, tight fitting sweaters, and slits in their skirts that came up to their thighs. Most covered their hair with brightly-hued scarves, no matter what they were wearing.

By the end of the evening, many of those lovely dresses would be soaked in sticky semen, the result of the "contraception" that Somali women used. Modern contraceptives were not available here, except for the rubbers that most men wouldn't wear, so Somali women had developed a different technique for ensuring that they did not get pregnant, for pregnancy would have interrupted their lives as hookers and destroyed their hopes for marriage or emigration. Using this technique, Somali women allowed men to shove their penis between the woman's thighs, with no penetration. With her thighs held taut, he would ejaculate, often staining her dress, but she was unlikely to get pregnant. Somali women also used wads of cloth soaked in oil and inserted like a tampon, to prevent pregnancy, but the "no penetration" technique was the most effective. A bonus to the "no penetration" method is that it kept intact the threads that had sewn a girl's flesh together, theoretically healing the butchery of a clitorectomy.

At the Lido what really set the Somali girls apart was their demeanor. Some took on the role of ingénue, holding back against the wall, keeping their eyes lowered a bit. The lowered eyes did not come from their culture; rather, they lowered their eyes imitating European and American women who used that affectation in movies. Other girls flaunted their availability, parading in front of the men. The ones in the parade tended to be a bit older, with perhaps a face wrinkle or two. A few women kept more true to themselves, holding their heads high and their backs straight, gazing over the room with a sense of power.

I watched Jeffrey, a Peace Corps volunteer, as he stalked one of the ingénues. First he stood at the bar, his back to the bartender, puffing out his chest, just staring at a young woman. She glanced up at him a couple of times, then lowered her eyes again. He sauntered over to her, as if he owned her, standing in front of her like the Marlboro Man. He took her hand, expecting her to follow him onto the dance floor. She resisted, but he insisted, pulling her behind him. The band was playing "It Was a Hard Day's Night," and they both bobbed and twisted to the music, he much more vigorously than she. Her moves may have been subtle, but they were ever so sensual. She was no ingénue.

There was a woman in a gold sparkly tee top who caught my attention too. As with most Somali women, she wore no bra, her natural curves just filling out that tee nicely. She wasn't waiting for someone to choose her. She found her target, then stood next to him at the bar. She was one of those gifted women who knew how to mold her body to fit into a man's contour, hardly moving a muscle. They were sort of facing each other and when he put his weight on his left foot, she shifted ever so gently to put her weight on her right foot, mirroring his actions. She was an absolute master at this. They kept nudging closer and closer, and soon he took her to a table in a dark corner.

At first I found this whole mating dance funny. Indeed, who was the stalker, and who was the prey? I knew very well that Jeffrey's target would not go home with him this night. No, she would play a teasing game. After all, she professed to be a virgin, and a virgin would not go home with a man upon first meeting him. No, she would wait a night a two before going home with him. Then, in a week or two after they had met and been intimate, she would break into tears and tell him how her family had disowned her because she was seeing an infidel. He, feeling guilty, would of course take her in and care for her. In the event that he felt no guilt, she simply returned to the Lido and began again. How was it, I wondered, that women know this mating dance so well, and men hadn't a clue? I decided that they didn't know because they didn't want to know. All they wanted was sex, no matter how they got it.

"Kansas City, Kansas City here I come" broke out over the loud speakers. Indeed, most of these women would give anything to go to Kansas City or Albuquerque or London or Constantinople, or anywhere their ex-husbands or family couldn't find them. Most of the women hoped for a free dinner this evening. The lucky ones would find a regular boyfriend who would meet them here from time to time, buying them meals and trinkets. Once in a while a woman would find a boyfriend who would support her for a few weeks, or a few months, either at his house or at hers.

The ones who caught the gold ring on this runaway merry-go-round were the ones who found marriage, especially marriage to a foreigner, which meant they could leave Somalia and begin a new life of comparative luxury, no matter where it was. The ones who were blessed, the tiny fraction of those truly blessed, would earn enough money to start their own small businesses, live independently and get out of this rat den.

Jeffrey and his prey were dancing to "Pretty Woman." Damn, I hated that song. It extolled the glory of whoredom, women whose sole purpose in life was to please men, women who had nowhere else to go. In a deep conversation about reincarnation, a guy once told me, most conspiratorially, that he would be a hooker in his next life, as if throwing yourself at a man for his sole pleasure was somehow a desirable life, an honor even. It astounded me that any man could consider whoredom anything but dismal.

Looking at these girls, I knew it was a degrading life for them. It was the end of the rope; it was desperation. If they couldn't make it here, they became gutter beggars, slowing starving to death. The deep sadness behind their eyes spoke so sharply of marital beatings, of losing children to sickness and abuse, of losing their own families when they couldn't tolerate their arranged marriages. Many of these women were married off when they were still children, perhaps only ten or twelve years old, to old men, men who had more camels than compassion. The camels paid their bride price; the lack of compassion fell on the women's backs with beatings and heartache. Now, banned from their prior lives, whether by divorce, death or escape, disowned by their family and friends, they sought new lives here, many of them simply surviving day to day.

Jeffrey's girl was dancing, weaving her hands in front of her, rather like the motions of a praying mantis, like the ones I saw at the Catholic mission garden.

Looking around the room at the hunger in men's eyes, I felt revolted. It was disgusting how western men, including Peace Corps Volunteers, could have sex with a woman when they knew that they could never give her pleasure. Many African men were raised with this concept, the knowledge that sex was solely for their own pleasure, and accepted it on the basis that this is simply how it is. But western men were not bred with that notion. Western men theoretically were raised with the idea of pleasing a woman, and there is no way in the world of pleasing a woman when her vagina is bone dry from a clitorectomy, when all feeling has been ripped from between her legs. She might feel pain, perhaps lots of pain, but she would never feel pleasure. As I looked around the room, I hated every man there.

It was time for me to leave. "Wild Thing" was bouncing off the walls as everyone shouted and clapped in time. I glanced over at Jeffrey and his girlfriend, dancing forehead to forehead, her hands still circling, and I remembered a small lesson I had learned in biology class a long time before, that a female praying mantis devours the head of her lover, sometimes even in the act of copulation. Somehow that gave me a sense of satisfaction.

I lowered my eyes as I left, ashamed for having ventured into this corner of Somalia, for letting my ego get away with me. There was nothing I could do to help these women. They already knew more than I would ever know.

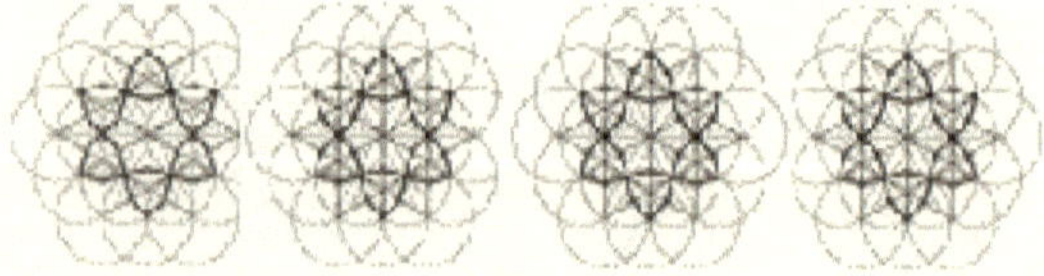

"My Mother, Her Sister"

"I long for you, like one
Whose dhow in summer breeze
Is blown adrift and lost."
(Somali song)

"HOW MANY TIMES have I searched this same dark alley?" I wondered. There were hundreds of similar streets in Mogadishu. This wasn't the street I was looking for.

I knew about searching dark alleys, finding hidden coffee houses and bars where the gay and lesbian community found itself. I knew the haunts of San Francisco, San Diego, and even Rome. I knew there was a hidden corner in every city in the world.

But I couldn't find that corner in Mogadishu.

There were no bars in this strict Moslem country, so I searched for coffee houses and cafes where women might congregate. I wasn't looking for Somali women. I vowed that I would never again inflict pain on any Somali woman like the pain that I inflicted on Shiamsa. No, I hoped to discover a community, however small, of European women, and perhaps even find one special woman.

When the stars aligned, when the roads were open and my teaching load of 50-plus classes a week eased up, when a bus or lorry was going into Mogadishu on a Thursday afternoon ... when all of that happened I got a brief interlude in the city, returning to Baidoa late Friday afternoon. I felt rather like a truant, skipping school for an adventure, but in truth I only made it into Mogadishu once every couple of months.

Friday was the Moslem day of rest, so while most stores were closed on Friday, lots of vans and lorries made the journey, transporting hundreds of travelers from town to town. There were no trains, and no busses, in Somalia. The rusty, dusty old lorries with peeling paint, piled high with goods and produce, with people piled on top of that ... these lorries were the backbone of Somali commerce. When I rode in a lorry, I was usually offered the seat up front with the driver, a much more dignified ride than the hayride in back. The lorries lumbered along the pot hole infested dirt roads, rocking like an old weary camel. There were ten-seater vans too, which I preferred – the ride was smoother, and jack rabbit sprinted along the path. There were no travel schedules. When a van had ten passengers, it took off, and the lorry drivers seemed to run on their own personal schedules.

So when the dirt roads hadn't been hit with heavy rains, and I could get to a departing van or lorry in time, I headed off to Mogadishu for an adventure. I wandered the streets of Mogadishu for hours, peeking into nearly forgotten coffee houses and cafes, sometimes searching the oceanfront.

Today was unique. There had been no classes at the Catholic orphanage on Thursday afternoon, so I left Baidoa at noon when the classes at Sheik Awes Middle School were over. The speedy driver in the van got us into Mogadishu in record time, sprinting along like a gazelle, so here I was, wandering the streets of Mogadishu on a Thursday afternoon.

A chill swept across the air, a foreboding of the rainy season that was fast upon us. I reached into the pocket of my sweater and felt the crunch of a piece of paper. It was a note I had written to myself months ago, to remind myself to visit the shop of Mussa Hasan's aunt. "My mother, her sister," Mussa Hasan had told me. I didn't want to have favorites at school, but Mussa Hasan was one of my favorites. Mussa bungled his way through most lessons, but he always wore a grand smile. Mussa had written down the name and address of his Aunt Sagal in Arabic under my own note, knowing that others would help me find her shop. I usually arrived in Mogadishu too late on Thursday evening, and the shops were closed on Friday, so I hadn't had a chance to visit "Aunt Sagal," until now.

After walking through a dozen twisted tiny streets in the old Arabic quarter of Mogadishu, I stood at a crossroads of about five alleyways. Down each narrow street, as far as I could see, were tall white stucco-finished buildings, two, three and even four stories tall, all hugging each other for stability. If one of them ever tumbled, they would all crumble to the ground. Since they had stood like this for centuries, I suspected they would stand erect for one more afternoon.

I don't know if it was my look of befuddlement, or that I simply looked out of place, but a very nice Somali woman in a bright pink and blue traditional Somali dress came over and looked at my piece of paper.

"*Ha!*" *Yes!* she said, smiling broadly and beckoning me to follow her. Within minutes we stood in a small shop, the shop keeper a bantam-weight, feisty, joyous middle-aged woman. Here was Aunt Sagal! In my limited Somali I told her I was Mussa Hassan's teacher in Baidoa and that I had come to say "Hello."

Aunt Sagal smiled even broader, if such was possible. She cleared off a stool for me to sit on and ordered messengers to bring tea and biscotti. Within a few minutes a full tea party began with Aunt Sagal's friends and neighbors congregating for the festivities.

The women were all dressed in brightly colored fabrics – reds, golds, purples, every color of the rainbow –with floral patterns and helter-skelter stripes and zig zags, some fashioned as traditional Somali dresses, and some as simple European style dresses with long gathered skirts and high neckline. All had glorious head scarves and multi-colored shawls. I felt like a withered onion in a vibrant petunia patch, for I was wearing only my plain pale blue skirt and long-sleeved shirt.

Women came and went, with eight to ten squeezed into the shop at any time. One woman, a secondary school student, stayed at my elbow, translating as best she could as several conversations converged on us all at once.

"You're from California. Do you know Roy Rodgers?"

"Why did you come to Somalia?"

"Do you know Miriam Hussein? She lives in Baidoa too."

"Do you wear these clothes in America too?"

"Do you like Somali tea?"

One woman brought her young daughter, a student in elementary school, who wanted to talk with a "real American". Her mother beamed with such pride when her daughter and I had a sweet little conversation.

"Do you like stories?" I asked this enchanting child.

"Yes! I like stories!" she said, with a wide grin and clapping hands.

"What is the best story?" I asked her. The secondary school student had to translate that question for the child, but her answer burst out.

"Arawello! I like Arawello!"

I couldn't help it, I simply scooped her up in my arms for a twirling hug. "Me too!" I said.

There were very few female entrepreneurs in Somalia, and Aunt Sagal was a special woman indeed. When her husband died, she didn't want to re-marry, so she took her modest savings and opened this little shop. The Somali government had a program where small shop owners like Aunt Sagal could buy goods at wholesale from large stores, under the condition that the small shop owner would not under-sell the large store. As part of that program, Aunt Sagal had been able to stuff her shelves with canned goods, imported tins and boxes from Egypt, India and Kenya. That program, and her captivating personality, won her a loyal cadre of clients, enough to support her four children, enough to ensure that five of her grandchildren could emigrate to the United States or Canada.

I tried to buy some aromatic Darjeeling tea and a box of brown sugar, but other women jumped in to pay for them, so I opted to not purchase anything else, and focused instead on our wonderful conversations. It seemed that no sooner had we begun than the *iman* from the local mosque sang out his call to all the men for evening prayers through his elaborate sound system. We said quick "Amana Allah" goodbyes as the women scurried home to prepare the evening meal.

The smile that I left with carried my spirits for many weeks to come. Quite unexpectedly, a few days later when I was back in Baidoa, Mussa Hassan ran up to me, positively grinning from ear to ear, telling me how happy "my mother, her sister" had been that I stopped to see her.

THE NEXT DAY was Friday in Mogadishu. I woke early, for this was the time I gave myself a special gift: the view of the sunrise over the Indian Ocean. A quick ten minute walk put me on the edge of the Indian Ocean. Mogadishu streets were deserted – the women were busy settling into the day while the men went to morning prayers.

I sat alone on the white sand, watching the sun barely creep over the clouds on the horizon. Shams, the Arabic Goddess of the Sun, dipped her brushes in iridescent pinks and tangerines, outlining the clouds on the horizon, creating the silhouette of a magical land where only fairy folk could go. This City of

Fairies shot gentle streams of light, as from a coloring book. Then, within seconds, a huge fiery opal burst forth, too beautiful to be real. The sun was alive, magical, on this day. I knew it was real, for I had seen this miracle before. Here was the original inspiration for this land of poets, the natural beauty that led them to burst into song. Sadly, my Somali was never good enough to hear the lyrical poems extolling the sound of a camel bell, or the majesty of a single tree, or the grace of a golden earring on a lady's ear, but watching the mystery of the sunrise I knew where the poetic gift came from. The lyrics wafted in from the sea, mingling with the sun's rays bursting across the countryside.

I glanced behind me where the early morning light encased the white buildings of Mogadishu in a crystal dome, gifting Mogadishu the sobriquet "The White Pearl of the Indian Ocean."

I breathed in this moment for an hour or more, the ocean ebbing and flowing to refill my senses, then I rose to find a café for breakfast and wandered the streets, some streets that were new to me, and some that I had visited before. I wandered past my favorite bookstore, but since it was run by an Arab, it was closed on Friday. I peeked in the window and made a mental note to stop by next time I was in Mogadishu – there was a new book of Somali poetry that I wanted to read. The Arab goldsmith shops were all closed too, and their alley was deserted. A bit of wandering more, and I found myself in front of my favorite Italian-run shop, and I immediately stepped inside.

"Maria!" I called out to the middle-aged woman arranging a shelf. Her bright red and green gathered skirt, with her white peasant blouse, spoke to her Italian heritage.

"Maria!" she called back, for that was the name she had given me. Maria stepped off her ladder and ran over to give me a huge hug.

"Cappuccino, no?" she asked.

"Cappuccino, yes!" I replied. This had been our greeting since we first met several months earlier.

Maria had already cleared off our corner of the counter and started our cappuccinos. As she reached into the cupboard for a tin of biscotti, I asked her how she was, how her family was, and what was happening.

"*Cosi tanto!* So much!" she said as she sat down on one of the stools, motioning me to the other. "As for me, I am wonderful," she said with a big smile as she waved a biscotti over her head. "Antonio, not so good. Maybe I should have married a younger man, but Antonio, he is so good to me. I think I will send him to a doctor in Nairobi."

"Please give him a big hug from me."

"I will," Maria promised. She paused, dipping her biscotti in the cappuccino. "But that is not the worst."

"Maria, tell me, what's the matter?" Maria never complained. I couldn't imagine what was so bad.

"I am not sure," Maria said slowly. "What it is … I am not sure. But something is happening in Mogadishu. People are nervous. They don't talk to each other when they come into the shop. They are serious, even the Italians and the French." She shrugged her shoulders, not knowing how else to explain it.

It would be several months before I understood what Maria was trying to say, before this discontent reached Baidoa in full force. The elections, which were still nearly a year away, were the root of the political discontent throughout the country. Every tribe, every town wanted the power that the office of President of Somalia held, and there would be over fifty candidates run for that office. The views of these candidates covered the whole political spectrum, from peaceful coexistence to immediate warfare with all who opposed Somalia, with lots and lots of variations on the theme. Some were decidedly anti-American and anti-European. Each candidate had a platoon, or army, of extremely loyal followers, all of whom were deeply passionate, even fanatical, about their candidate's position. Any kind of compromise was not an option. Even in Baidoa coffee shop conversations had broken into nasty physical fights already. It would only get more intense as the time for the election drew nearer.

"But you are okay?" I insisted.

"*Si*. I am okay," Maria replied. Taking a deep breath, she continued, "And I have some special things for you today!" Maria brought out tins of chocolate, green olives, black olives, garbanzo beans, coconut, rich coffee beans, and all sorts of goodies that I just couldn't get in Baidoa. She even had a jar of maraschino cherries! When I filled up my own tote bag, she gave me one of hers so I could stock up to last over the rainy season.

Maria and I hugged for an extra long time as I was leaving that day, and I am glad we did. Antonio passed away soon after my visit, and Maria returned to Rome to her family. We never met again.

Before leaving Mogadishu, my last stop was always the ice cream shop, the only ice cream shop in all of Somalia. I sat and savored my vanilla ice, the only flavor that was offered, pondering this very special visit. A few other people came and went as I sat there … a young Somali family … a group of French children … a German couple … but not the woman I was looking for.

As my van pulled out of Mogadishu that afternoon, I looked back longingly, still searching. I knew that she was there, the woman I wanted to know. She had to be there somewhere, but I still didn't know where. It would be nearly three months before I could return to Mogadishu to search again.

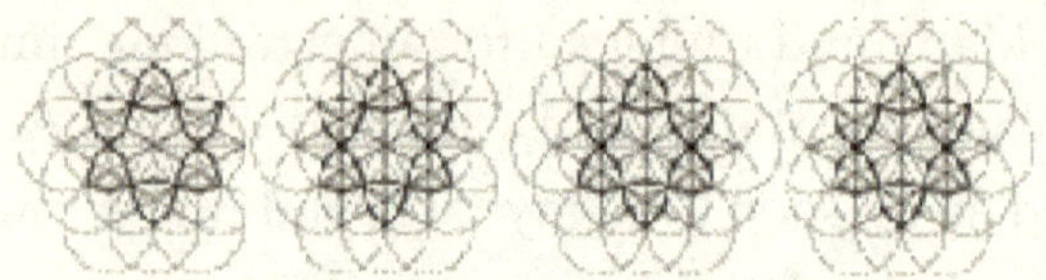

His Crazy Wife

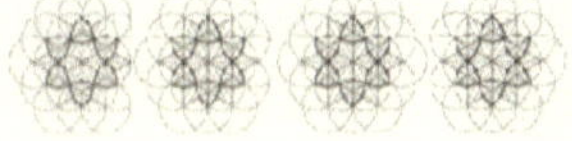

SHE SAT on the four foot tall fence in between their house and the café next door, keeping a good eye on Tom, the Peace Corps volunteer in Lugh, a village on the border of Ethiopia. After all, Tom and all his friends came and went from that café every afternoon. The fence was the adobe divider between the two properties, and it had a nice flat surface she could sit on. She watched them drink their afternoon tea and eat their meals. Sometimes it seemed that Tom and his friends were there forever, but her attention never faltered. She knew that she wasn't welcome in the café, and took all of her meals at home.

The Somalis called her *Xaas Waalan* ("Crazy Wife"), for only a Crazy Wife would devote such attention to something that didn't concern her.

Tom had found her on his doorstep one afternoon, a scraggly little grey kitten, all alone. Her mother had been killed trying to steal of speck of meat, her siblings were gone. Tom took her in and patiently fed her milk with a rag soaked in goat's milk. Gradually she got better and better, and ultimately adopted Tom as her mom. And she watched over him as he sat in the café next door.

When Tom stood to take his evening walk around the village, Xaas Waalan jumped off the fence and took her place at his heels, just in case he wanted company.

"Hey, Tom," shouted Habiba, the waitress. "Where's Xaas Waalan?"

Crazy Wife flicked her long grey tail, holding her head high. She knew very well where she was.

When Tom left the village the following year, he left Xaas Waalan with a boy, a good student, and provided money for her care. Tom discovered later that some of the village men had taken Xaas Waalan to the desert and left her there. They had no use for a frisky little kitty.

There is a tale in Somalia about why cats prefer women. It is not because women are kinder, although they usually are. It is because women are the powerful ones in a household, and cats like associating with that power. Sadly, there was no woman nearby to rescue Xaas Waalan that hot afternoon when those village men snatched her off the street.

A Crack in the Bamboo Curtain

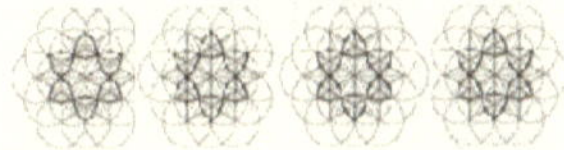

VIBRANT RED POSTERS appeared all over town, on buildings and schools, announcing the performance of the Chinese dancers just a couple of nights hence. Abdi, the headmaster, tore down the posters tacked onto Sheik Awes Middle School.

I was intrigued. This was four years before President Nixon would break through the Bamboo Curtain, opening up Chinese ping pong tournaments and cultural exchanges. When I saw those posters in Baidoa, we knew woefully little about modern China, except that we were enemies. The Chinese culture was truly a mystery. Here was an opportunity I had never even dreamed of, to see real Chinese dancers, perhaps even to meet them.

Somalis designated our modest house as the Hospitality House for any non-Somali passing through. According to Somali custom, any relation, whether previously known or not, must be afforded all the consideration of an honored guest with housing, meals and conversation. So whenever foreigners showed up in the region, they ended up on our doorstop, a serendipitous bit of adventure that I really enjoyed. We hosted a Norwegian student hitch hiking through East Africa, an Argentine photographer on assignment from National Geographic, and even a Belgian couple on an exploratory mission for the United Nations. I felt honored that it was our modest house – not the larger, richer houses of the USAID staff or the Mennonite missionaries –our house was the "Hospitality House" of the region.

But no Chinese had shown up on our doorstep. Somalis knew the Chinese were different, and had not brought the Chinese dancers to our house.

The teachers at Sheik Awes Middle School told us not to go to the performance. Even the Regional Governor told us not to go, but my curiosity simply could not contain itself. I was sure I would never have another chance to see real Chinese dancers. "Besides," I rationalized, "what danger could possibly hide in dancing?"

I soon found out.

As two of the agriculture Peace Corps volunteers and I entered the courtyard of the elementary school where the performance was being staged, we were offered bright red buttons that the Somali ushers were passing out. One button showed the bright red Chinese flag, the other showed the US flag in flames. We declined the buttons.

Instantly a circle closed in around us, six tall men, each man sporting a holstered gun and the tan uniform of the Somali police. They formed nearly a complete circle around us as we stood in the middle of the two hundred or so Somali men pressed into the courtyard for the evening's performance. Everyone had been checked at the door for weapons of any kind so we didn't see what danger could possibly lurk in the dark corners of this closed courtyard. But we didn't turn away the police protection.

We were accustomed to being the only white faces in the middle of the audience, just as we had been at the local cinema. Tonight brought "entertainment" to a whole new dimension in Baidoa.

As a grey dusk fell, lights sputtered on in the courtyard. A strong marching beat spewed from drums and cymbals, and from the sides of the plain raised platform marched a dozen dancers in red pajamas. I couldn't tell if they were men or women, and it likely didn't matter. I expected the performers to leap into synchronized gymnastics, but it didn't happen. They marched. As they formed basic patterns in their marching, they were each handed a Chinese flag and a wooden rifle, both of which they waved wildly. A large Chinese flag rose as a backdrop behind them as they saluted it with the intensity of a Nazi *"Heil, Hitler!"*

Then everything changed. The spirited march evolved into a wild death dance. They traded their Chinese flags for a good size American flag. They spat on the American flag, shot it, stabbed it, ripped it apart, flung it to the ground and stomped on it, digging it into the ground like a spent cigarette butt.

Anti-American sentiment roared in that courtyard.

"Kill 'merica! Kill 'merica!" Then louder and louder as more joined in the chanting. The chants bounced off the walls, the sneers of angry men boring holes into us. The protective shield of policemen closed ranks, their hands on holstered guns.

Had it not been for the police guard surrounding us, I quake to think what might have happened. It was past time for us to leave. As we began edging our way to the door, the police didn't break their protective shield. Two of the policemen stayed with us and escorted us home.

I couldn't believe that President Shermake would allow this kind of performance, an invitation to violence. It had to have been arranged by a dissident political group. When I asked some Peace Corps volunteers in other towns what they thought of the

Chinese dancers, they told me that no Chinese dancers came to their towns. I hoped that the dancers were evicted from Somalia after their performance in Baidoa, but it seems more likely that they were affiliated with the Chinese who had just finished building a large theater in Mogadishu for live performances, along with other construction and training projects that the Chinese provided to Somalia.

Those flashy red buttons popped up all over Baidoa the next week or so, but there wasn't a single one at Sheik Awes Middle School – Headmaster Abdi wouldn't allow it.

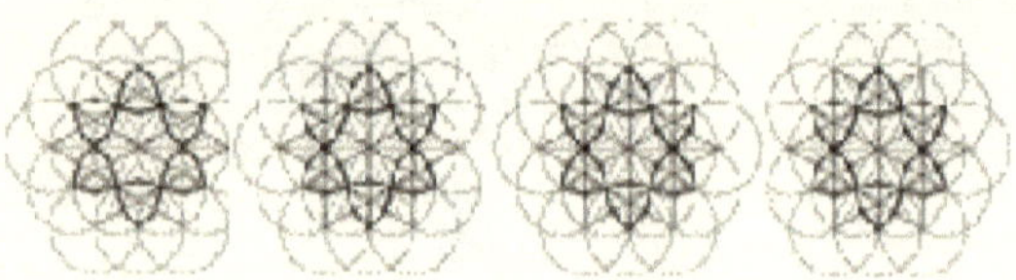

Draft Boards and Bullets

When asked to explain a man's bedspread, a wise young woman said, "A man's bedspread is Peace, For with Peace he can sleep anywhere."
(Somali saying)

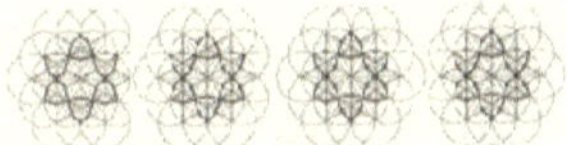

"DRAT, I WISH they'd draft me!" Lefty slammed his fist on the table, startling both Stu and me.

The three of us sat at my dining room table, a game of penny ante poker in progress. Yes, Lefty would rather be drafted into the U.S. Army than serve out his term in Somalia. Lefty was a pre-med student, a sharp young man. At least in the U.S. Army he could serve in the Medical Corps, while here he was teaching farmers how to plant in neat rows. "Lefty" in fact wasn't even left-handed. He simply swung a bat as a left-handed batter, and so the name "Lefty" stuck.

Draft boards were alive and well during the late 1960's during the Viet Nam War, with power hungry little bureaucrats putting the lives of young men on the line, forcing them to go slaughter strangers. Conscientious Objector status was hard to come by, with those so designated working in the medical corps or at menial non-combative positions.

Each local board decided for itself how to handle Peace Corps volunteers. Some boards gave full military service credit for Peace Corps volunteering, taking the young man's name out of the eligibility pool entirely. Some gave deferment, taking his name out of the pool only until his Peace Corps tour was over. Some boards ignored it, demanding that the names of the young men remain in the pool, and if their name came up, they were pulled from the Peace Corps to be drafted into the Army. It was this latter group that Lefty was in. He knew he could be called back at any moment, and at that moment he wished he would be called back.

Stu sat pensively. Stu had already told us about how he had broken curfew and nearly been shot. Stu was returning late from visiting an outlying farm and didn't even know there was a curfew that night.

"Yeah," said Stu, "I know what you mean. That Somali Army guy was serious – he wanted to shoot me!"

Stu wasn't kidding. The curfews were imposed by the central Somali government, an effort to curtail rumored uprisings. I didn't see any actual uprisings in Baidoa, but the curfews were imposed on the whole country nevertheless.

And that was indeed the order to the Somali Army: Shoot on sight, no questions asked, if anyone is found outside their homes after 8:00 pm. Anyone. That meant Peace Corps volunteers too. The fact that the Somali Army was trained by Russians, our defined enemy by any measure, didn't soothe our souls.

Just that afternoon Lefty and Stu had come in from their lone posts to pick up supplies in Baidoa, and another curfew was announced. These curfews were irregular, and very spur of the moment. We didn't know what prompted them, or who in fact called the curfews, except that it was someone very high in government.

It was late in the afternoon that day, around 5:00 pm, when the curfew was announced, and neither Lefty nor Stu wanted to get caught on the road after curfew, so they were bunking at our house. When the order is to "Shoot on sight," you don't take chances. The Baidoa Police, who were trained by Americans, were always very protective of Molly and me, making a special trip to our house to personally warn us of impending curfews, but even they could not have stopped a Somali Army bullet.

"So what did you do when the soldier threatened you?" I asked Stu.

"I begged," said Stu. "I did - I absolutely begged. Fortunately, the Army guy knew enough English to let me go." I could imagine Stu's wild blond hair blowing in the wind, pleading that he was not Somali and was not part of this political situation, whatever it was.

We had also heard from Slim the previous week. Slim, a volunteer in a lone post, had scrunched down by himself one night as several people were shot just yards from his front door. His mud hut wouldn't have provided much protection, but it was all that he had.

"Yeah," said Lefty, "it's a whole lot safer in the Army than in the Peace Corps."

Rumors were flying fast and furious that a civil disturbance of some kind was coming; some called it a civil war, some called it a revolution. None of us knew exactly what it meant, except that we didn't want to get caught in it. Earlier civil wars in Somalia had wreaked havoc akin to the Battle of Gettysburg, but for decades longer … bodies bursting with guts spewing out year after year. The Peace Corps guys only half -heartedly teased me about my edgy nerves, for their nerves were edgy too.

"I asked our chief in Mogadishu about the situation when I was in there a couple of weeks ago," said Stu.

"What did he say?" I asked.

"He said they would let us know if anything important happened," said Stu.

"So what is considered 'important'?" I asked.

"Dunno," said Stu. "He just didn't say."

So on this pale evening we lit the gas lantern, closed the window shutters, and played some penny ante poker with matchsticks.

"I'll meet your rotten little penny and raise you two more," said Lefty, flourishing his three matchsticks.

"It's three cents to me, and I'll do it," I said confidently, knowing full well that I didn't have a chance of winning with a pair of fours.

SHUUUUU POP!

A single shot rang out in the dark, much too close for comfort. Stu was closest to the lantern and immediately blew it out. We fell to the floor and knelt in silence for a good ten minutes. Nothing else happened.

"Well, it's time to hit the sack anyhow," said Lefty, very softly.

"Yeah," said Stu.

"Yeah," said I. But none of us moved. I crawled to the front door and opened it just a hair, reassuring myself that Omar Chicago's son was on duty. He was. And he was quite alert, crouched down, unmoving in the dark, poised to leap. He held his hand on his dagger, with the dagger half out of its sheath.

We crouched down by the poker table in silence for another half hour before any of us dared to make a single sound. Then, without saying a word, we each rose quietly and went to bed.

I asked around the next day to find out what had happened. No one seemed to know, not even Omar Chicago. Or perhaps no one would tell me.

I told myself that I didn't really live in a war zone, and in truth that was the only shot I heard fired in Baidoa, but it was just too close, too real. My jagged nerves just got more skittish. This was not the Peace Corps that we bargained for. Granted, one bullet does not make a revolution, but that bullet echoed for a very long time.

We waited. We all waited. Days passed, one after the other, sometimes wet, sometimes hot and dusty, but mostly mild and warm. The electricity in the air was caused not by violent weather but by the lurking violent undertone of fear … an ill-defined raw fear of what might be coming, and deadly curfews for reasons unknown.

Bikini Flambé

A flash of lightening does not sate thirst.
What then is it to me if you just wander by?
(Traditional Somali love song)

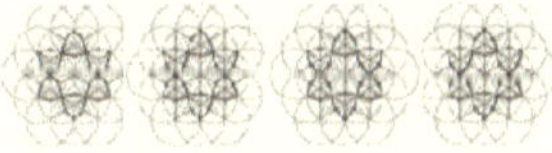

I STRETCHED TALL, a luxurious reach to the powder puff clouds, all five foot three inches of me, revealing a taut bod in a tiny pink and aqua striped bikini, and I let out a small moan to welcome the sun. I heard a low whistle behind me.

"Who the heck is that?" said the guy who whistled

"Dunno," said the guy next to him. Two male volunteers were lurking, and yes, pre-bikini they knew me.

But now I certainly didn't look like anyone they met in Peace Corps training. The oversize shirts and loose wraparound skirts that I usually wore as a poison pill to ward off unwanted advances bore no resemblance to these teeny bits of fabric, and it felt good! In fact, it felt great!

We were on the long verandah of the American Club, a small beach resort on the Indian Ocean on the outskirts of Mogadishu. It was a squat building, about two thousand square feet, finished in white stucco, conspicuous only by being the sole structure on that stretch of beach. Somalis didn't swim, or fish, along this stretch of beach so here we were alone, and here is where we literally let our hair down. Here is where embassy staffs and ex-pats from the United States, Italy, France, England and the western world gathered to play.

It did appear that someone sent out a memo to all the Western embassies saying, "No Negroes Allowed in Somalia," for there were none. I never saw one Black face at the American Club. There was the occasional Hispanic, but not one Negro. And the only Somalis here were the cooks and maintenance staff. Even the 24-hour guards were white Americans, Marines mostly. So we had our lily white playground all to ourselves.

I didn't visit the American Club often, and when I did go, I felt like an interloper from a different country, for it was all so foreign to Somalia.

THIS BIKINI ADVENTURE began abruptly when George, a Peace Corps volunteer stationed in Mogadishu, barged into my seventh forum class about 11:00 am a couple of days prior. He must have left Mogadishu early to get there before noon. His demand was simple and direct: " Get an overnight bag, we are leaving NOW."

Good heavens, was the civil war starting? The thought chilled my spine. Tensions were rising rapidly – more curfews and more fights, both verbal and physical. One of the Somali teachers had taken me aside a few mornings prior and told me quickly, "You must leave Somalia now. It is not safe for you." None of us knew how much longer we would be able to stay in Somalia. This sounded like the end.

It was early, so if we rushed we could make it into Mogadishu before any curfew hit. George so startled Molly and me that we didn't stop to ask the why or wherefore. We knew we had to get out.

Quickly dismissing our classes, we hopped in George's van for the ride to our house at Omar Chicago's compound. No one at Sheik Awes Middle School questioned that we had to leave. They looked as stunned as we did. Molly and I each packed an overnight bag, and hopped in the van. I only had two changes of clothes, my brown skirt/blouse and my blue skirt/blouse. I was wearing one, so I quickly packed the other, not stopping for niceties. George had already picked up Frank, one of the other volunteers in the region, and the four of us sped off.

I tried to scrunch down in the back seat as we left Baidoa. The sound of that sole bullet that disrupted our poker game a few weeks earlier still rang in my memory.

We were headed to Bur Hacaba, the village at the foot of Bur Hacaba Mountain, that odd mountain that stuck up like a sore thumb in the middle of nowhere.

"Why are we going into Mogadishu?" I ventured.

"You'll have to ask Jack, our fearless leader," said George. "All he told me was to go get you and bring you in … pronto."

Molly and Frank and I exchanged knowing glances. So this is It, the revolution is beginning. I braced for whatever might come.

We sped over the rut infested dirt road, the strange Bur Hacaba mountain getting closer and closer. Bur Hacaba was a true anomaly in Somalia, a tall 300-foot mountain, about 400 feet in diameter, that sprang out of nowhere. It just sat there, in the middle of thorn bush country, all by itself, with no other mountain in sight. There was a legend that a vile wizard lived atop Bur Hacaba, capturing maidens for his pleasure. That tale no doubt evolved just to keep women off the mountain.

I once saw Bur Hacaba from above, an experience I never wanted to repeat. At the end of summer school in Baidoa, the rains had us trapped, and miraculously the Peace Corps sent a small prop plane to take the four of us to Mogadishu so we could begin our vacations. We were leery of the pilot before we even began. He was a Somali, and as we boarded the plane, he took out the pilot's manual, which was in Italian. As he opened the pages, we sincerely hoped that he knew how to read Italian, for none of us did. We sat stunned as he actually started the plane and took off. None of us had had time to act on our collective thought: to abandon ship. As we flew near Bur Hacaba, this manual-reading pilot opted to take a nose dive at the mountain, "so we could get a closer look." He missed hitting it by a few feet only, and with my guts in my throat, I couldn't even scream. Blessedly, we did make it into Mogadishu in one piece, but we landed only after he flew around for half an hour, waving at all the other pilots in the air that afternoon.

As our Land Rover bumbled into Bur Hacaba village, George mentioned that he had actually spent the prior night at Buddy's house, so Buddy was expecting us. True to form, Buddy, the Peace Corps volunteer stationed in Bur Hacaba, had sandwiches and cool water ready for us as we pulled into his compound.

"I've got the basket packed," called out Buddy. "Let's go!" I expected Buddy to jump into the van, but George and Frank jumped out of the van instead. Buddy grabbed the picnic basket and they headed off.

"Are you girls coming?" called George as they sped off down the path in the direction of the mountain.

Confused, Molly and I followed. Buddy and George led us up to the side of Bur Hacaba Mountain to a small path winding up the gentle sloping side. About half way up the mountain, the path made an abrupt turn, and in front of us was a lovely pool of water surrounded by boulders and greenery, a surprising little lagoon about fifty yards wide.

"Where did this come from?" I inquired, rather dumbly.

"It's their water supply," explained Buddy. "They have barrels in the village, but this lagoon captures the rain and holds it for the dry season."

Within seconds, George, Buddy and Frank were gleefully swimming nude in the small reservoir. It didn't strike me as odd that we had stopped to pick up Buddy. It did strike me as absurd that the guys went swimming nude, and at a time like this. This little reservoir was a natural one, created in an accumulation of boulders. It captured rain water for the village below. This was the only source of water for the village for months on end. No wonder women weren't even allowed on the mountain – on the offhand chance that menstrual flow contaminated this reservoir; the whole village would suffer for months.

"Come on, girls!" shouted George. "Don't you know how to swim?" Molly stripped down to her bra and panties, both of which soon became transparent in the water, laughing outrageously at the boys' antics. I was the fuddy duddy standing nearby.

"I thought we were in a rush," I called out.

"We were," called George. "We had to get here so we had time to swim before dinner." Jeez, I felt like a dumb dolt. I had jumped like a terrified rabbit when George told us to get out of Baidoa, never stopping to ask why. I still didn't know if the revolution was part of the equation, but I was beginning to doubt it.

"Do Somalis swim here?" I naively asked, for there were none around.

"Heck, no," said George. "They're not smart enough."

I was simply disgusted. This was the drinking water for the whole village for heaven's sakes. And Buddy's participation surprised me. Buddy was a decent lad, a Yale graduate with some class. Maybe Buddy was just trying too hard to be one of the guys. I called out a good by, skittled down the mountainside by myself and looked for a lorry going into Mogadishu. I was fed up with all of them.

I found a lorry ready to leave. The driver jumped down, ordering the man seated in the passenger seat in the cab to get down and ride in the back of the lorry, then regally offered me that seat.

"For you, teacher," he said proudly.

"You!" shouted the displaced man, the one who had been in the passenger seat in the cab. I turned to look. "You!" he said. "'merican?"

"Yes," I said smiling. "I am a teacher in Baidoa." I spoke in my best Somali.

The man scowled, turning his upper lip into a sneer. He spat on the ground. "This lorry for Somalis, no 'mericans!" He started to climb back into the cab.

I stepped back. "I will find another lorry," I told the driver.

"*Maya! Maya!* No! No!" said the driver, quite sternly. "You sit here." He pointed decisively to the passenger seat in the cab, motioning for me to get in. Four Somali men jumped down from the back of the lorry, ready to defend the driver. A policeman appeared too, likely the only policeman in this village. The policeman broke the tension, making sure that I left safely with the lorry, while the disruptive man was held behind. The rest of the trip was mercifully uneventful.

When I got into Mogadishu, I found out that, at least as far as the Peace Corps was concerned, the revolution was not starting. All that the Peace Corps wanted was my paperwork for a civilian passport and attendance at a two-hour de-briefing session with a dozen other volunteers. In the de-briefing session everyone put on a happy face and said how great their tour was, when we all knew that the happy faces were for the tour of duty ending, and for going home to the

States, not for the memories of the past two years. It seems that this little session had been planned for months, but no one thought to tell the bush volunteers about it ahead of time. Having completed this very unimportant business, I opted for a proper swim in the Indian Ocean.

I had to admit that the tiny bikini surprised even me. I had never in my life worn a bikini, let alone looked great in one. But here I was, looking fabulous.

That morning Julia, my traveling companion a few months earlier, had gone with me to look for a bathing suit so I could enjoy the brilliant sunshine at the American Club. She was heading back to Kismayo to meet her fiancé, the USAID guy, but she had a couple of hours free to go shopping. We found a small shop run by an Italian woman that catered to European tastes. I picked out a nice blue one piece suit. Julia picked out the bikini for me, saying that if she looked that great in one, she would get one too.

Two weeks later Julia was summarily kicked out of the Peace Corps. She had the gall to marry the USAID guy, the one she had been seeing for over a year. As long as they were shacked up, all was well. But heaven forbid they should get married. Peace Corps rules forbade marriage, so off with her head!

I attributed the great bikini look to the fact that I had probably lost in the neighborhood of thirty pounds while in Baidoa. Our diet was a bit less than meager – heck, I felt guilty eating chicken, for honestly those chickens needed food more than I did. I suspected their eggs, which we ate each morning, were just as emaciated. We had virtually no veggies or fruits. A mango or papaya was a rare treat. We did have some stringy, chewy camel meat from camels too old to carry a load anymore, and sometimes old goats or cows. The meat was nearly always in chunks in a tomato paste sauce served over rice or sorghum-based spaghetti and didn't even vaguely resemble my Tia Sophia Bongiovanni's lasagna or sauces. Somalia had abundant frankincense and myrrh, befitting the legendary land of Punt, but it didn't have a single oregano bush that I could find. Even Mogadishu didn't sport so much as one café worthy of the title "trattoria."

And we were sick. Good heavens, were we sick. In spite of our weekly quinine regimen, we all got hit with malaria several times. And the dysentery was unreal. One night Molly and I were both so sick with dysentery that I had to crawl from the bedroom, across the living room to the front door, leaving a trail of stinking brown gunk staining the cement floor behind me. One of Omar Chicago's sons was always stationed outside our door, and I begged him to go get the missionary nurse.

Another time Molly came down with a massive case of malaria that shot her temperature over 105. There was no way of reaching the Peace Corps doctor in Mogadishu. Our only direct communication with

Mogadishu was via the short wave radio talks at the USAID station in Baidoa, scheduled for each Monday and Thursday. This was Tuesday. I asked Omar Chicago's son to go ask the Mennonite missionaries if one of them could come by, and when he discovered that they were out of town, he ran over to the Catholic mission and asked for Padre Vittorio's assistance. Padre Vittorio showed up in a Police Land Rover, loaded up Molly and me and drove us to the Catholic mission. Moments after we arrived, a second Land Rover pulled into the courtyard with the Russian doctor, the one assigned to the Army base. The Russian doctor no sooner saw us than he tried to get back into the Land Rover, but Padre Vittorio and Mario wouldn't let him leave.

Through the convoluted translations that day, i.e., the doctor's Russian was translated into Somali which was translated into Italian, which Mario translated into French for me, which I translated into English for Molly. After all of that, we uncovered two important truths: (1) the Russian doctor was terrified that Molly would die and headlines around the world would proclaim "Incompetent Russian Doctor Kills Young American Girl Peace Corps Volunteer"; and (2) the Russian doctor had determined that the traditional dose of quinine just didn't work anymore in that region, that the mosquitoes had become immune to it. The Russians began using something very different, which had no translation at all.

A couple of weeks later when I explained the quinine situation to the Peace Corps doctor in Mogadishu, he pooh-poohed it as third world chicanery. So I asked Padre Vittorio if he would ask the Russian doctor if he had enough of the new meds for Molly and me, and the very next day big bottles of it were delivered to our house. I never knew what it was, the labels were in Russian. But it worked. I dug into my private stash of goodies that I had brought back from Mogadishu, and I made one of my incredible three-tier chocolate cakes, sprinkled with chocolate chips and coconut, to thank the Russian doctor. Nothing could have thanked him enough for keeping malaria away from our house. I wish I could have given him a headline that read, "Compassionate Russian Doctor Saves American Peace Corps Girls." But I couldn't. So the chocolate cake had to suffice.

SO WITH THE lousy diet, the dysentery and the malaria, here I was, on the veranda of the American Club, looking out over miles of pristine white beaches, the afternoon sun caressing nearly every inch of me.

And I was hungry. One of the true joys of the American Club is that we could get real flame broiled hamburgers, dubbed "beef burgers" out of respect for our Moslem hosts who wouldn't touch "ham" or "hamburgers", with loads of ketchup, mustard, mayo, pickles and even lettuce with an audible s-h-k-r-i-t-c-h, onions and tomatoes. That, and a big plate of French fries and a Coke, cost about fifty cents. I was so grateful to the American embassy for arranging this little bit of paradise.

I turned to get my beef burger and saw her. Her long dark hair flitted about, tickling her breasts and her bright yellow bra. Her thumbs linked over her red cutoffs, pulling it down to show her strong, smooth belly, while curvy legs – runners legs -- flowed from the fringe of her shorts. And her eyes. Oh my goodness, her eyes … they were dark, and much too big for her face, and they looked straight into me. She leaned against the doorway in a practiced casual stance, one foot raised alongside the knee of the other leg, showing off crimson toenail polish. For months and months I had searched Mogadishu, coming in every chance I got, looking for a woman whose company I might treasure. There were none. None. I finally gave up, resigned to being alone for the duration of my tour. Then this beautiful creature kept looking at me, looking into me. I was afraid to believe that she truly might be interested in me too.

She smiled, just a little, a quizzical, inviting smile, the left side of her mouth curling up to reflect the arch of her raised eye brow. I smiled a bit too, and nodded just slightly. She peeled away from the door, a bird of paradise unfolding. Jeeze -- my crotch was wet, and my knees were too whooshy for me to move. I had been hoping beyond hope that I might find someone like this, so why couldn't I just walk up and say, "Hello"?

Just as she leaned to take a step toward me, a man's hand reached around the door frame and stopped her. This large, tall muscular man whispered something in her ear. She glanced at me and tried to say something, then turned and followed him out.

Sorry? I was just kidding? Later? Oops? What was she trying to say? I couldn't read her expression. I saw an embassy sedan pull out of the driveway, but I couldn't see who was in it, or what flag flew on it. Maybe she was someone's secretary-on-call at one of the embassies. Or someone's whore-on-call. Or the wife of some junior staff person. Whoever it was who had called her away, I was just plain ticked off. For a few moments it had been such a provocative little fantasy.

I stuck around the American Club later than I should have, just in case … then I caught a three wheeler taxi back to the hotel at sunset.

Actually I was looking forward to this evening. The very beautiful, and very stylish French Ambassador's daughter was throwing a party, and every young ex-pat in southern Somalia was invited, as well as all the Peace Corps volunteers.

My Peace Corps pal Eddie had created a cocktail dress for me for this event. Eddie and I had become buddies back at Columbia University when we both did student teaching at the same school in Harlem. In its infinite wisdom, the Peace Corps assumed that teaching in a black ghetto somehow prepared us for teaching in Somalia. In truth, the connection between American Blacks in Harlem and Africans in Somalia was at best pretty flimsy, and in terms of my Somali students' ability and motivation, the Peace Corps should have sent us to advanced academies for our student teaching.

But there we were, student teaching in Harlem. The route for Eddie and me from Columbia University to our school passed through Morningside Park, a notoriously dangerous area, so I was glad for Eddie's company. Eddie was of slight build and logically could not have protected me against a gang of thugs, but he walked with a stride that said, "Don't mess with me, bastard," and no one ever bothered us.

Eddie and I never discussed our private lives, but I did notice that he went to The Village every Saturday night to visit a male friend, and we didn't see him again until Monday morning.

Eddie was a fashion designer by profession, so naturally he was assigned to be a teacher in Mogadishu. Fortunately, he had been there but a couple of months when he hooked up with the weavers in Mogadishu and began working with them. The weavers functioned like a European guild, all working in the same alleyway, all creating individual lengths of cotton cloth in stripes and plaids on custom looms. Eddie was helping them develop a market in the United States for their unique fabrics.

Eddie relished the notion of creating a cocktail gown for me in just two days, and with his contacts in the fabric world of Somalia, he made me feel like an enchanted Cinderella. Eddie didn't use Somali cotton for my dress. No, he chose a marshmallow soft periwinkle China silk and fashioned it into a Marilyn Monroe inspired halter style, the front panels crisscrossing my breasts, a full skirt accenting my tiny waist, and the hem just above the knee to show off my trim, gently tanned legs. A couple of yards of bluegreenturquoise flowered China silk created a shawl, with a bit of that fabric left over for a snug ribbon tied at my waist. The silky fabric totally washed me in bewitchery, especially since I wore no bra and no stockings. There were no buttons or zippers, just elastic at the waist so I could slip into it, and made it easy peasy for the tailor to pull together.

THE FRENCH AMBASSADOR'S residence was much like the other embassy homes, but more so. It was a large two-story box building surrounded by a ten foot tall wall, guards at the gates, no terraces or patios for outdoor life. It was life in a box, albeit an expensively decorated box.

The French had quite a tenuous relationship with Somalia. During the prior century Somaliland came under the control of five different nations, as represented by the five-pointed star on the Somali flag. Two sections – the northern British section, and the southern Italian section – had joined to form the Somali Republic in 1960, with the goal that all five sections should be rejoined. The unification of all five points of the star was a mantra throughout Somalia.

But two sections – the sections in Kenya and Ethiopia – were ceded by the Europeans to the neighboring countries, creating constant border wars.

And the fifth section was Djibouti, a tiny section at the northern tip of Somalia. Under French rule Djibouti had become more prosperous, stable and diverse than any of the other sections, and when the Somali Republic invited Djibouti to join it, Djibouti declined, turning the Somali Republic's five pointed star into a mockery. Djibouti became a tiny country unto itself, a bit of treachery that Somalia never quite forgave the French for instigating.

I had not met Sylvie, the French ambassador's daughter, but the instant I walked in I knew who she was. Her blond, softy wavy hair, with her Grace Kelly style and Vogue inspired cherry pink gown set her apart from everyone else. She was simply stunning. I couldn't say the same for the Peace Corps contingent. The boys in their beige slacks and white shirts, and the girls in cotton frocks didn't hold a candle to Sylvie's style, nor to mine.

The party was in the ballroom of the French ambassador's residence. Somali homes, even the homes of the wealthy, were typically austere. The

French ambassador's home was anything but austere. The exquisite artwork and statuary in the ballroom needed no excuse for simply being there. The parquet wood floors had no doubt been imported, as were the embossed wall coverings. Like most embassies, the French provided generators for their staff accommodations, so the crystal chandeliers shone brilliantly.

I didn't know if I wanted my bird of paradise to be there or not. She was indeed beautiful, but she also appeared to be with a man at the American Club. Perhaps my desperation had really mucked up my judgment. I reprimanded myself for even glancing over the room to see if she was there. She wasn't.

I sidled over to the tables holding the promised "light refreshments," piled high with thinly sliced marinated beef and smoked turkey breast, and cheeses – brie and camembert -- and sourdough bread, fishes, salads, hors d'oeuvres, a cornucopia of exotic fruits and signature French desserts. A whole table off to the side created cherries flambé, with a coterie of guests waiting. Another table held only the finest French wine. I barely got a taste of a herring morsel when I felt her behind me, an eclectic energy igniting every strategic spot in my body. Then her strong hand rested on the small of my back. My bird of paradise had found me.

"You look *tres chic*, Moriah. But I liked the bikini better."

How did she know my name? I stiffened my back and decided to play it very cool. I turned slightly to see a striking woman in a black satin pantsuit with a yellow and white striped silk tee, elegant in its simplicity, hugging her ample breasts just enough to show off taut nipples. Her dangling gold earrings were created, no doubt, by the goldsmiths of Mogadishu. Her long hair was pulled to one side, with huge dark waves tumbling over her shoulder. She was taller than I remembered from seeing her that afternoon, and she absolutely took my breath away.

"I'm afraid you have me at a disadvantage," I said quietly. "You know my name, but all I know about you is that you are very beautiful." My cool had melted.

"My name is Jani." Her undulating French accent put the emphasis on the second syllable. "Jani du Lac." She paused only briefly. "There is a door in the corner behind us, on the right. Meet me there in five minutes. No … make that two minutes."

Jani didn't wait for my response, but merged into the guests, apparently looking for someone. I treated myself to a tiny chocolate éclair and a sip of champagne, then made my way to the designated door. The door was slightly ajar, so I opened it enough to slide through, closing it behind me. I stood in a narrow corridor. Jani was already there, about ten yards away, talking with that same man. My face flushed with anger – What was he doing here? Why did he have to intrude on our very personal rendezvous?

"Okay, Jani," was all that I heard, and he disappeared into a hidden door.

I put my cool back on. "Your husband?"

"No, *cherie*, not even my lover. Robert is my boss." She stood close, her hand tracing the outline of my face. "I am a body guard for Sylvie. I am sorry I had to leave this afternoon." Her fingers traced my eyebrows and my nose. "We heard a rumor of another curfew being announced, and the embassy gets very nervous when that happens. So we had to return here." Jani gently tilted my chin, and our lips met. There was no more pretense of being cool. The soft crème brulé sweetness of her lips pressed us ever closer.

"*Mon dieu*," she whispered, then took my hand and led me down the hallway, up a flight of stairs, and into a room of golden shadows.

Silks and satins mingled while an eider down comforter lifted us on tangerine clouds like a magic carpet, tumbling onto the sheepskin rug where we tussled to taste each other.

"No, no, *cherie*, don't challenge a black belt." So I didn't.

The kisses of my French lover were the sweetest I had ever tasted. We spoke little. I asked about an erotic embroidery she had on her wall, and Jani told me the story of a woman she met in India who created this image from the carvings of the Taj Mahal. I hoped that one day I might be able to give her something that she treasured as much as that embroidery.

"How long have you been in Somalia?" I asked.

"On and off for the past three years."

"How long will you be staying?" Now that I had found Jani, I didn't want her to leave. I had flashes of us visiting the romantic sights of Europe together.

"Five minutes … or five years," Jani replied. "We never know." I felt the urgency in Jani's voice, an echo of my own feelings. Nothing in Somalia waited for lovers. The best we could hope for was a few exquisite moments together.

When I reached to unbutton her slacks, she took my hand and savored each fingertip hungrily, as though each fingertip were covered in nectar. Then she dusted my neck with her kisses, slowing finding her way to my breast. Tauntingly, she stroked my tummy and traced the edges of my panties. She knew exactly what she wanted, and so did I.

BANG!BANG!BANG! – the door shuddered under the powerful pounding. "Jani! *Vite!*"

"*Sacre bleu!*" Jani screamed. "*Non!*"

"**Oui**!" demanded the man's voice, Robert I assumed. "*C'est Sylvie. Vite!*"

Tears flooded my eyes as Jani leaped to put on workout pants and pull on a tee.

"Stay here," she whispered desperately. "I'll be back." In a few seconds she was gone.

What could possibly have happened that would pull Jani away from me? Screw Sylvie – she had looked just dandy a few minutes earlier in her prissy pink gown. There were noises all up and down the corridor, footsteps, doors opening and closing, men's voices and women's. I couldn't pick out Jani's voice in the melee.

Then silence.

At first I let the silence envelope me in the eider down comforter, and I breathed deeply, smelling Jani pressed to me. I glanced out the window and the whole city had turned to a grey still life, sharp corners casting mauve shadows on the alleyways. I tried recapturing the rapture, running my own fingers from my neck to my breast. But it was no use. I didn't want me. I wanted her, all of her. I wanted the strength of her devouring me, pushing out all the memories of the past two years, leaving me spent, baptized anew. It was not to be. I finally slipped on my China silk dress and wrapped myself in my shawl, a barrier against the chill, and settled into to the silence.

After a while Robert appeared, a pale silhouette in the door, motioning me to follow him. We went down the hallway to a panel that opened up to a narrow stairwell. At the bottom Robert left me with another French guard. We drove through unlit back alleys of Mogadishu, our car lights dark, and I instinctively covered my hair and face with my shawl. He saw me to my room at the hotel and made sure I was safe. Then he left. Not a word had passed between us.

My heart screamed for answers. Where was she? Who was she? Was she safe? Could we be together again? But there was no one to ask, and there were no answers.

I ran across other Peace Corps volunteers the next day, everyone praising the fabulous party, especially the champagne. I seemed to be the only one who knew that something unusual had happened, a fact that I kept to myself.

I stayed in Mogadishu as long as I could, but I knew she wasn't there. The impending rains forced me to leave Mogadishu lest I get stranded away from Baidoa for weeks. The long slog back to Baidoa took over fourteen hours, stopping every few minutes to push the van out of yet another slushy pothole.

Back at Omar Chicago's house I got a message sent via the short wave USAID connection. It had arrived a few days earlier, and it said simply, "We are in Djibouti until Friday -- J". Dammit, it was already Thursday, and the blasted roads were totally washed out. I could barely get out my front door, the torrential rains having created a six inch deep lake for several hundred feet around. The tiny airstrip was washed out too, so even if I could get hold of a private plane, it was of no use. I was trapped. My tears got lost in the downpour, my heartache did no good at all.

Several weeks later when the roads opened up, I fled back to Mogadishu, to the French ambassador's home. I begged the guards to please give my little message to Jani du Lac, but they claimed to not know the name. They said no one of that name ever worked for the French embassy. And when I mentioned Sylvie's name, they turned me away completely. They wouldn't even take my note.

I wandered for hours. I walked the desolate cold beaches until all I could see was the white foam skipping over the breaking waves. The bitter wind lashed out, tossing shards of sand at my face and legs.

I went back to the French ambassador's house to beg one more time, but this time the guards wouldn't even let me inside the gate.

I never saw Jani again. Jani was gone.

Gone.

Elegy for Eddie

My mouth is bubbling
It is telling me to speak
(from "Deyn Maayo Heesaha" by Hadrawi, a
Somali poet exiled because he wouldn't follow
orders to write only patriotic songs. Written in
1973.)

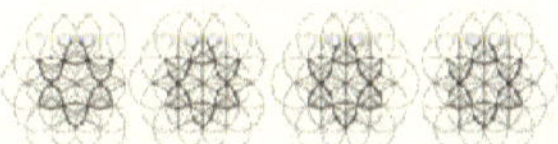

I STOOD outside the Peace Corps office building in Mogadishu, rain pouring down, shouting **"I AM A LESBIAN!"**

The rains had kept me sequestered in Mogadishu for four days. There wasn't much to do but drink tea in the daytime, and get drunk on rot gut wine at night. That afternoon I was sitting at a tea cafe with a steaming cardamom tea and a biscotti when I overheard a snippet of conversation between two male Peace Corps volunteers behind me.

"Hey, Don, did you hear about Eddie?"

"No, what?"

"He's gone home."

It was true. I hadn't seen Eddie for a couple of days now.

"But we've only got a few months left."

"Yeah, Jack said it was for medical reasons."

"He was a fag, wasn't he?" They guffawed in a shared secret.

"Yeah. Yeah."

The wave of sadness that I felt was for the Peace Corps, and for Somalia. Eddie was a talented, creative volunteer. The burst of rage was for Eddie … and for me … and for every other volunteer who had to tolerate the Peace Corps' idiotic rulings.

I had to shout at someone, so I shouted at Jack, the head of Peace Corps in Somalia. I stood out in the street, shouting at the window in his office.

"DAMMIT, YOU FLEA BITTEN JACK – CAN YOU HEAR ME? I AM A LESBIAN!"

Burt, the assistant country director, ambled out of the front door. "You're going to have to do better than that if you want us to pay your way back home." He spoke, clipping his consonants like a BB gun shooting at a tin can. He grinned. "Heck, you don't even look like a dyke." He walked past me, and kept on going.

"By the way," Burt called out as he tipped his hat, "Jack is in Hargeisa."

Ritual

Allah, forgive my sins …
Allah, forgive my sins …
Allah, forgive my sins …
(Moslem prayer)

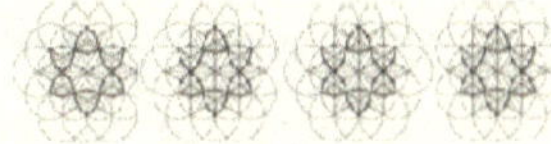

I WOKE UP, gasping for breath, my face burrowed into the pillow, stifling my screams. The first time I felt this dream, this nightmare, this terror, I woke up Molly and Omar Chicago's entire household, screeching into the night, so I had moved my personal belongings into the second bedroom, the one we used for guests, and tried to muffle those night terrors.

The dream began simply on a spring-like afternoon that lured me into a walk into the bushes like a siren's song. I followed a camel trail just wide enough for one or two people. Scrub bushes had burst into bloom for a few days of glory. This was very different from the incredible blooming of the Anza Borrego Desert near my home in California, where carpets of pink-blue-purple-white wild flowers burst into life as far as the eye could see. This was a gentler spring; small white, blue and yellow flowers peeked out midst the thorns. Swallowtail butterflies with blue and green bands flitted about, navigating around the small yellow and multi-colored ones. One blue banded butterfly tickled my nose, no doubt curious what this strange flower was. I even caught a glimpse of a skeletal Praying Mantis like the ones that flitted around the bougainvillea bushes in the village. Other bugs and butterflies were no doubt busy at their springtime work.

My tour in Somalia was coming to an end and I had not taken a single walk in the countryside, the heavy teaching load was always in my way. Today, on this beautiful sunny day of my dream, the little path jumped up in front of me, inviting me to follow it. I must have passed that part of the road dozens of times, but I had never noticed this path before today. I settled into a quiet walking meditation, something I hadn't gifted myself for a very long time. I thanked Allah for the beauty of this land, and for the kindness of its inhabitants, human and non-human alike, and I asked the Deities to protect it from danger as one protects a growing child. "Give it room and time to grow as it will," I asked.

From an echo out of nowhere rang a scream that froze my spine, a girl's voice screaming *"MAYA MAAAAAYA ... AAAAIIIIIII!"* Then again. And again.

I ran toward that scream. The scream grew louder and more passionate as I ran closer, clearly the cry of a girl terrified. Thorns pierced my arms and hands as I pushed through the bushes, but I hardly noticed. This girl was desperately crying for help. For an instant I believed I could heal all the misery I had brought to Baidoa by saving this girl from whatever danger pursued her.

I stopped abruptly, for in front of me was a clearing with a single small hut. The ten or so women here walked with a determined gait, not a panicked one. The girl who was screaming was being dragged by two large women in the direction of the hut. Her arms flailed about ... her legs kicked as hard as she could ... her body dragged in the thorny dust. She fought them bitterly, but they held her tight, demanding submission. I knew this girl – she was Amaani, the little sister of Abdul Mohamud, one of my students. I remembered Amaani's dress, a unique shade of green with cheerful orange flowers. When I met her a few weeks ago she was a joyful young girl, about ten years old. Now she was a screaming maniac, fighting as though her soul depended on it.

Sometimes in my dream Amaani escaped, fleeing into the bush with a speed and agility that the older women didn't possess, her dress ripped by the vicious bushes in her way.

But not this day … not this nightmare.

Off to one side were two girls sitting with an older woman, singing and clapping softly. I couldn't see their faces, but it appeared to be a surprisingly serene corner of the tableau before me.

On the other side was a large mat where three girls laid. Two of the girls were curled into a ball, desperately clutching each other's hands, crying uncontrollably. The third girl laid quiet, her mouth open, her eyes shut – she didn't move. The mat was soaked in blood.

NOOOOOOO. The protest came from so deep inside me that my universe shook.

The older women saw me and immediately formed a protective shield, holding out their shawls so I couldn't see what was going on. One woman who was holding a large shard of broken glass started toward me, the weapon over her head, ready to strike.

I turned and ran … I ran for my life … I ran from the horror … I ran for the safety of my girls … I ran as I didn't know I could run. Thorn branches attacked me from every angle, my bloody arms attracting all manner of bugs, my face covered in disease carrying blood sucking vermin. I ran until I could run no more, then collapsed on the desert floor, pain shooting through my belly to my head and to my aching feet, my fingers too bruised to bend. A whirlwind of thorn branches caught me in their grasp, beating me unmercifully as the realization swept over me that I was The Snoop who had seen too much … I was the Superior One who wasn't part of this ritual … I was the Helpless One who could do nothing. I held my knees, rocking back and forth. NO! I didn't see that – NO! I don't want to know that… NO! it didn't happen … the sun tricked my eyes … the devils of the bush country conspired to transport me somewhere else … I didn't see it … I..didn't see it … I …didn't …see .. it. It had happened to someone else … just not me.

I had heard of clitorectomies, the ancient African practice designed to obliterate any trace of sexual sensation in beautiful young women. Women in many African societies carried out these rituals so that they could be "clean," be "pure" for their husbands by eliminating the sticky lubrication that women produced during sexual contact. Uncircumcised girls were considered "unclean" and were ostracized from proper society. Uncircumcised women were filthy. I was filthy in their eyes – no amount of bathing would ever make me clean.

I remembered Amaani, and Jamila, her mother. They were such a loving, even affectionate, family, with Amaani so proud to help her mother serve tea for my impromptu visit. Jamila's pride shone in her warm smile. When I saw Jamila in my dream just now, her face had turned granite hard, drained of its lovely subtle coffee tones, for it was Jamila who wielded the shard of glass. Her eyes burned chills down my spine. In truth, Jamila deeply believed that she was acting out of complete love for Amaani in performing this procedure. As a "filthy" young woman, Amaani could never hope to find a husband. She had to be made "clean."

I hated Jamila for what she did to her daughter Amaani. I wanted to tie Jamila to a tree and let her skin parch in the blistering heat, desert birds pecking at her skin, but I knew that there was nothing I could do to Jamila more painful than what she had already endured, for she had had a brutal clitorectomy too, as had her mother and her mother before her, back hundreds – perhaps back thousands – of years. No one knew when or why this ritual began, or when it would end. It was simply a given that each generation of women had to inflict the same barbaric procedure upon their own beloved daughters, knowing well the agony it brought.

And yet, Jamila's eyes – there was something else there.

I had let myself believe that in Somalia a clitorectomy was an antiseptic little procedure, like a Jewish boy's brit, a simple snip snip and it was over. But in this nightmare it was no antiseptic procedure. Even in other Somali tribes, the ritual might not have been so brutal, the pain blurred by special herbal applications. But here primitive shards of glass and rusted blunt knives inflicted unimaginable pain as every iota of the girl's clitoris was ripped out of her from between her thighs, scraping the labia clean as well; then the vagina was sewn tight, leaving but a tiny hole for her menstrual flow and urination, preventing entry for years to come, until her wedding night. If a girl didn't die from loss of blood, she could die from the infection that ensued, or from the excruciatingly painful childbirth a few years later.

I knew that girls in backward tribes deep in the African jungle were still assaulted with this brutal procedure, but not girls in Baidoa. Not my girls. Not my beautiful smart kind girls. Now I knew that my beautiful girls would never know the joy of a human touch; for them, sex was to be endured if they could manage intercourse at all, or sexual contact was stripped from their lives forever. I searched my memory, looking for an escape from the pain, but there was no escape.

I kept seeing Jamila's haunting eyes, beyond the granite glacier wall of first glance. There was something else there. There was a plea for understanding.

What was I to understand? That she could brutalize her own daughter?

I wanted to believe that I would never bring pain to my daughter, but I knew that if I had been raised in an African village, I would follow the customs of that village, especially if my daughter's future depended on it, much as Chinese mothers hobbled their daughters with brutally painful fractured feet for uncounted centuries. Who was I to judge?

I cared, yes, I cared deeply. But I had no right to judge. One moment I wanted to toss Jamila's honey drenched body into a hill of killer ants; the next moment I simply wanted to hold her and tell her everything would be alright.

I vomited everything that was in my stomach, and more, slowly coming to realize that I had no idea where I was. I had abandoned the path long ago, and now I couldn't see over the tops of the thorn bushes to find my direction. So I sat there, lost, for what seemed like hours, too afraid to call for help, too afraid to make my presence known.

As dusk began to fall I saw the heads of several camels waving over the bushes about twenty yards away, and I ran to intercept the nomad band.

"Where is Baidoa?" I humbly asked. Heavens above, I must have looked a wreck, my clothes ripped, my arms, legs, face bloody.

"There," said the man in front, pointing behind him. He kindly poured water into my cupped hands, once, twice, then three times, easing my parched throat.

With the sun at my back I staggered home, arriving long after the sun had set on this, my most horrifying day in Somalia. I learned later that a curfew had been called that night and it was purely by the grace of Allah that I wasn't seen … and shot.

I rarely made it through the whole nightmare before screaming myself awake, just as I had that night.

I was awake very late that night, praying to Gods and Goddesses whose names I didn't even know.

"God, forgive my sins …
Beloved Goddess, forgive my sins …
Spirits of the universe, please forgive my sins
Forgive me for presuming to be superior to Jamila.
Forgive me for condemning a woman who would give her life for her daughter."

Jamila simply knew no other way. This was the tradition; this was the African ritual, just as it had been for as long as anyone could remember. There was no luxury of choice, no "Choice A" or "Choice B." It simply was. If she wanted happiness for her daughter, it had to be. I made a promise deep in my soul, so deep that I wasn't even aware that I was making it. I promised that one day I would do something to help Jamiila have a choice.

Amaani's screams still echo in my ears, even now, nearly half a century later, and sometimes I still wake up with my face buried in my pillow, my useless cries muffled, night terrors still flooding the dark.

"God, forgive my sins …

Beloved Goddess, forgive my sins …
Spirits of the universe, forgive my sins

Then, tomorrow…

Fatuma, one of my stellar students, the one who stood by herself most mornings, stopped me as I walked to school. I had never seen her on my road before. She had come out from behind a tree and stood before me.

"Teacher." She paused, gathering her courage. "Teacher, I am not cut. My daughters … I will not cut them."

The immensity of that statement brought tears to my eyes, just as I thought I would never cry again. I took Fatuma's hands in mine and squeezed them gently. "I am glad, Fatuma. I am so glad."

Baidoa, Somalia –
The Last Night

March 22, 1969

> *The Tree of Life*
> *A tree grows on the moon. It is the Tree of Life.*
> *Every time someone is born, a new leaf grows on*
> *that tree, and whenever someone dies, a leaf falls*
> *down.*
> *A Somali proverb.*

The proverb doesn't say what happens when a
country falls apart.

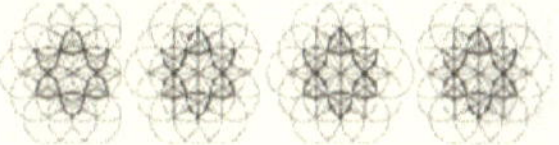

I STOOD by that mud puddle, a straggler fearful of what the dark held. The rain had stopped.

As I turned to walk down this path for the last time, a mist rose from the puddle, tear drops obscuring the stars, hiding all the world around. Out of this mist rose the beat of soldiers marching, hundreds of them, leaping African warriors, twirling machetes and rifles in the air. These Somali soldiers spread out over the countryside with determination like millions of army ants, setting homes aflame, leaving raped women and dead children in their wake.

…The women's cries reverberated over the countryside as their vaginas were ripped apart, tearing the stitches from clitorectomies, rupturing the flesh that had grown together.

…Mothers spread themselves over their children, shielding them from certain death, to no avail. When the mortality rate of infants was already over eighty percent, killing these precious children left a swath of grief-ridden villages across the whole country

…The sad weapons of the local Somalis were wasted, the men either joining the massacre or falling in wretched agony.

"NO!" I screamed. **"STOP! THESE ARE YOUR PEOPLE!"** But no one heard. I spread my arms wide, but the army marched right through my shadow. As the killers passed I saw flames that shot to the heavens, begging Allah for mercy, for rain to quench the fires. But there was no mercy this night, only piercing screams as souls escaped pained bodies, reaching for the afterworld.

So this is what the civil war looked like. I struggled to see which Somali war it might be, but they were all the same, each an internal combustion spewing madness.

The mist closed in on me again, only silent screams remaining. I reached skyward, begging Allah to help these people.

A pinpoint of light broke through the horizon, someone walking toward me, a silhouette against the dark. It was a woman holding a babe, with four other children clutching her tattered dress. As she slowly drew closer I saw that she wasn't alone. Hundreds – no thousands – of marchers followed her, each trudging through the relentless dust, all slowly walking

"Where are you going?" I dared to ask.

"To Ischia Baidoa, to the wells of Baidoa ... water ... water ..."

They didn't know ... they didn't know that even the Wells of the People had dried up, leaving blistering boulders in an endless drought. They didn't know that Baidoa, once *"Baidoa gannay"* ("heavenly Baidoa"), once a paradise on earth, had become The City of Death, the place where people came to die.

They kept coming … and coming … women … children … old people … the crippled … all weary, all hungry, all begging for a sip of water … putting one torn bleeding foot in front of the other, believing they would soon find relief. I walked up to one woman, her tattered dirt drenched dress barely covering her, a package of brown rags held fast to her breast, a babe's tiny face nearly hidden in the filthy bundle. But the babe wasn't suckling. I pulled back the rags to see bones poking out from shriveled flesh.

"Your baby is dead," I said softly.

"No," she replied. "Water … water." And she kept on trudging in line.

I curled up in pain by that solitary mud puddle. I had no tears left. I had no prayers left.

In the darkest hour of the night I glimpsed a ring of fires begin to flare, at first just a few then thousands of them, encircling the entire country, flames shooting higher and merging in a spiral dance. From the crimson flames of the dance rose a regal form spreading arms over the arc of the sky. Golden serpents wound round her arms. In a blink she was gone, leaving the star studded Royal Path, the Milky Way, in her wake.

As the rays of first light washed the world in grim reality, I saw the van sitting by Omar Chicago's place. It must have arrived during the night and had come to take us away. Oddly, I wasn't anxious to leave, but it was futile for me to stay.

The streets were quiet as we pulled out of Baidoa, the open air merchants just beginning to set out their wares. I saw a handful of my students, but none turned to wave. There had been no goodbyes, no *"amana Allah."* We slowed beside a large-framed man, and Luigi turned to see me. He smiled softly and touched the brim of his hat in gentle acknowledgement. I smiled softly too and waved gently. "Goodbye, my friend."

FOUR MONTHS LATER, President Shermake won re-election, but only two months after that he was assassinated by one of his own body guards, tumbling the Somali world, brutality upon brutality engulfing the country. The first few days every single foreigner was kicked out of the country. USAID, embassy staffs, missionaries, the Peace Corps – everyone – was given twenty-four hours to get out, many of them escorted to the planes in Mogadishu and Hargheisa by armed militia.

The droughts and famines came later, then again … and again.

Brutal civil war…devastating droughts and famines … pirates…invasion of the Black Hawks. Somalia was facing decades of challenges I couldn't begin to imagine. The naïve dreams I brought to Somalia when I first arrived were gone too, replaced by a prayer for her survival.

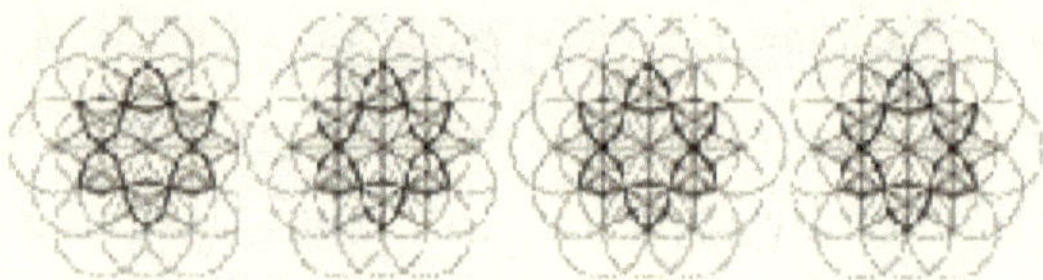

Lax

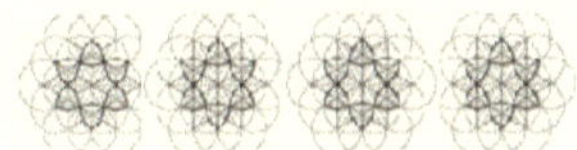

July 1969

I STOOD in the grand foyer of the United Airlines terminal at Los Angeles International Airport, watching the hundreds of travelers stretching their sight, seeking loved ones and lovers. After wandering the cobbled streets of Europe for three months, the long red-eye flight from London left me spent. I was ready to go home.

There she was. "Mom," I called out. "Here I am."

I stooped to pick up my big basket, the one that contained all my worldly goods, as she walked toward me. But she kept on walking past me, her sights on another redhead about twenty feet behind me, a spirited young woman. My mother did not recognize me.

The daughter she was looking for was gone.

I stood there empty, like a room that is to be re-painted, everything gone or covered up. No chairs, just a tarp stained with others' blood. No tears … until now.

So come … Sit. Sit beside me. Let us speak of queens in the mystical land of myrrh.

Amana Allah,
Miriam Yahr

Dear Reader,

While most of the characters in THE MYSTICAL LAND OF MYRRH are purely fictitious, there are two based entirely on real people: Padre Vittorio and Omar Chicago. I cared very much for both of them since they were both very caring people. I have learned that Omar Chicago was killed, fighting in the Civil War that erupted in 1969.

But with all the hundreds of contacts that I have, I have not been able to reach Padre Vittorio. I very much fear that the good Padre was caught in the devastation of the Civil War while trying to protect his boys. If you have heard of him, or of any of the nuns who served with him, of any of the boys who lived at his mission, please let me know.

Please join me at http://MysticalLandOfMyrrh.com for discussion topics and a bit more information.

The ongoing transformation of Somalia is nothing short of miraculous. The women of Somalia fuel the flames of that miracle. May our blessings go to each and every one of them.

Miriam Yahr at the green gate at Omar Chicago's house, 1967

Amana Allah. Go with God.

p.s. I truly appreciate comments from my readers.

Please go to
http://mysticallandofmyrrh.com/comments and you will see a handy link for commenting. I'd love to hear what stories you enjoyed the most, and which ones you least liked.

Thank you ...

These stories were written in deep love for the people I met when I was a Peace Corps Volunteer in Somalia from July 1967 to April 1969, and for those Somalis I have been blessed to meet since.

A special thank you to my dear friends Abdiazzziz Gulad and Miriam Foster. Abdiazzziz attended one of the schools that I taught at in Baidoa, and his memories have prompted so many splendid images and conversations.

And how do I thank Heather Cumming? When I needed someone who was familiar with African customs, she was there, and was so encouraging. Thank you so much, Heather.

Few writers are fortunate enough to have a coterie of colleagues like the Southern Oregon Women's Writers Group, Gourmet Eating Society and Chorus, but I have been. Special thanks to Bethroot, Madrone, Cyndi, Mary Beth, Tangren, Mara, Raynie and the dozen or so amazing early draft critics.

I was always so delighted when a friend appeared and asked, "Please, may I read the Somali stories too? Please?" These inspired readers gave so much inspiration and encouragement, and so I thank Mari and Nancy and Mary and all the other wonderful women who gave so generously of their time and knowledge.

You might also enjoy:

SOR JUANA, MY BELOVED: The Poetry, The Passion That Is Sor Juana Ines de la Cruz

This 17th century Mexican nun was blessed with extraordinary intelligence, and she had two passions in life: Poetry and the Viceroy's wife. Her courage led her to a confrontation with the Inquisition, where she stood firm to protect those she loved.

Moira, a young Peace Corps Volunteer, and a lesbian, confronts a magical, sometimes terrifying, land of Somalia. Ancient tales hold Somalia together, while modern warfare tears it apart. Moira quenches her soul at the women's watering holes, and in the classrooms of her students, while all manner of peoples -- local clan leaders, nomads, earthy waitresses, Italian ex-pats and the orphans of the Catholic sanctuary -- all pull at her energy. Over it all is the aura of Arawello, the Somali Goddess Queen, who once rose from Her people to save the nation, and who may do so again. So strong is the pull on her heart that in the end even Moira hardly recognizes herself anymore.

"It's a captivating read and shares a unique perspective. Nicely done!"
Barb Dickinson, *We'Moonager of*
WE'MOON DATE BOOK: GAIA RHYTHMS FOR WOMYN

"This has evoked such deep emotion in me. You have put pen to paper so eloquently and did the Ritual justice in all its darkness."
Heather C. Cumming, *Executive Director and Founder*
Simwatachela Sustainable Agricultural and Arts Program

About the Author

MaryAnn Shank has drawn upon her two year tour as a Peace Corps Volunteer in Somalia and turned it into a captivating story. A professional business writer, she has also contributed poetry and fiction to online sites and hard copy publications.

THE *Mystical Land* OF *Myrrh*